THE GOOD FAMILY

Ryan Licata

THE GOOD FAMILY

A JOE VELLETRI NOVELLA

Cover design by Hannes Pasqualini

First Edition

ISBN: 979 868 246 9703

No name. No memory today of yesterday's name; of today's name, tomorrow.

– Luigi Pirandello
One, No One and One Hundred Thousand

One

Although the sun cannot be seen, its light cuts a hazy outline into the city's concrete edges. The old widow drags her shopping cart through the market. The vendors greet her as she passes, buying her groceries as she does each morning: the strawberries and cherries, which are in season, picked in the hills of Trentino, and the last of the blood oranges from her native Sicily. Because it is Friday, she buys fish, a pair of sickly looking *trote* for her son's lunch. The fishmonger cleans them. As he cuts the heads off, the dead black eyes stare up at her, and she feels the weight of her own sagging, sun-spotted skin.

She misses Palermo on mornings like this, when the wives of fishermen fry calamari in the Mercato Vucciria, where women buy fresh what they cannot pick from their own herb gardens. *Pecorino pepato* and *ricotta di pecora, melanzane, sardine fresche, gamberi rossi*, all they need ahead of the weekend, when there is always cooking to be done for some *matrimonio, battesimo*, or *festa. Funerali*, too. The women share their news, sing their children's praises, or talk about what their men are doing or, rather, what they're not doing.

But Milan is not Palermo. The Milanese are like these *trote*. Cold and sometimes difficult to stomach. Even if they've known you for years. She's told her neighbours about her son's turn for the best. But they have their own ideas about him.

Almost home, back in the Chinese quarter, she walks slower up Via Paolo Sarpi. Despite the early hour, the little stores are lively, the shopkeepers *vivaci*. Men unpack green bottles from wooden crates. A cook beside a boiling pot of water chops chunks of meat with a cleaver. The Chinese always seem to be moving quickly, as if they don't want to be caught idle. Or they do not move at all. At the entrance to a small café, a woman sits at a table. Steam from a teapot rises in front of her, and she stares at it intently, as if it revealed her fortune. The widow tries to guess the woman's age. It's difficult to tell. The Chinese have such beautiful skin.

The Italian tailor, working from a stall hidden amongst the textile shops, lays garments out beside his Singer sewing machine. The rent in the Chinese quarter is cheaper. But still Italian businesses don't seem to last, a year at most before the tenants move along and newcomers arrive to replace them. On Via Paolo Sarpi, only the barbershop and old Tullio's bar have survived in the twenty years she has lived here.

Next door to the bar, a new bakery has opened. Family run. *Il Panificio Levita*. She slows down to get a whiff of the fresh bread. The lights are on and there is a queue out the door to purchase the warm brioche. The baker's wife comes out with a bundle of ciabatta loaves. She's wearing one of her bright headscarves. Yellow today. It suits her cheerful temperament. Her handsome son places the bundle with care into the basket at the front of his bicycle. He kisses his mother's cheek before pedalling up the road. *Che bravo.* Perhaps their business will last. She wishes them well.

But she does not stop. She needn't queue. These days, her son has the bread delivered, even if she doesn't see the sense in it. Why must she pay extra when she passes the bakery each morning? But Tommaso insisted. Unlike him, as he has never bothered with anything so domestic before. He doesn't even like bread. *Beh*, in her experience, people don't change, but if her son's habits have, all the better for it. Today she is grateful. Her legs are killing her.

She trudges the last stretch up Via Messina to their apartment. The pain from her legs shoots up her back. It seems to get a little worse each day. She wishes her husband had thought about the inevitability of old age before renting a place on the second floor. But he'd been both selfish and myopic. Not to mention stupid to think they'd be safe in Milan. She knows better. The Friends are as tenacious as *scarafaggi*.

She looks up at the apartment. The sun beats down on the white plastered brick wall. The shutters to the kitchen window are closed. She knows she opened them before going out. Tommaso must be awake. He never cared for sunlight. That's his father's blood in his veins. She can never have enough.

She leaves her groceries at the foot of the stairs but slips the fish, which needs to go in the icebox, into her bag. The rest can wait. It's only one flight, but she doesn't have the strength. Tommaso must help her. She hopes he is in a helpful mood. She goes up slowly, clutching the banister. She unlocks the door with the key she wears on a string around her neck. The house is quiet.

'*Tommaso, mi puoi aiutare con la spesa?*'

There is no answer.

She goes into the kitchen. In the dark, her son seems to be sleeping at the table. A shadowy bundle lies near his head. The bread has been delivered.

'Tommaso? *Che fai?*'

She puts down her bag, rests one hand on the table, gripping the key in the other. She shuffles to the window and opens the shutters to the sunlight.

Her son sits shirtless, slumped forward, his hands dangling at his sides. A chunk of bread fills his mouth. His face is bluish pale. And his eyes stare blankly at the brown paper bag of ciabatta loaves.

'Tommaso?'

Two

S triding up Via Paolo Sarpi, the detective raises the collar on his long overcoat and tugs his derby hat down just enough to shade his eyes from the sun. It may be summer, but Lombardy mornings still chill his old bones.

The address the boy Chupeng has given him is on Via Messina, only a few blocks from his own residence. He chose to live in the *pensione* on Via Paolo Lomazzo in Milan's Chinese quarter, because it seemed a good place to hide. At least from his enemies.

It isn't the first time he's had to keep his whereabouts a secret. In New York, he and Adelina had moved farther up-river, where he was less recognized, but not entirely unknown. On the streets of Lower Manhattan, he'd been respected by the people he helped but hated by those he tried to put away, or better yet, send back to the Old Country.

Now in Milan, he needs to lie low. But while he's forgotten, the scum continues to surface. And here, he's in the thick of it. With all the privately owned businesses, organised crime thrives in Chinatown. The Black Hand wearing it like a glove. The good thing is, with the stench of *mafiosi* on every corner, he seldom needs to ride the overcrowded trams. He can simply walk to work.

A young police officer guards the entrance to the apartment block. As if avoiding the sharp sunlight, the detective turns his scarred right cheek away from the youngster. A scar makes a bad first impression, especially on the police, who do their own share of scarring.

'I'm with the newspaper,' he says, touching the brim of his hat.

'Really?' says the officer. 'Someone's already up there from the *Gazette*.'

The youngster's face is freshly shaven. It looks red and sore.

'I'm with the *Corriere della Sera*,' he says. 'Chief Inspector Cattaneo alerted me.'

Hearing his superior's name, the recruit squirms in his tight-fitting uniform like a pup on a leash. He takes another look at the detective's hat, his overcoat, down to his black, polished, double-soled shoes. Then he steps aside and looks the other way.

The detective bounds up the stairs. He is short and bullish, but there is an almost lithe urgency in his movements. On the second floor, the heads of neighbours stick out from doorways but duck in again on seeing the gruff looking man in a winter coat and odd hat. He is more often mistaken for a criminal than a man of the Law. In the past, his peasant's features and stature have worked in his favour. People were more likely to take him into confidence, tell their secrets, and if not confess their crimes, then reveal the whereabouts of those who committed them. But times are changing. Now whether they take him for a *mafioso* or the police, the same rule stands. *Omertà.* Silence or die.

The door to the apartment is ajar. Inside, the living room appears poor but clean. Indistinct voices come from down the hall behind a closed door.

There is a sudden high-pitched ping, a flash of light, and a young man wearing a flat cap backs slowly out of what appears to be the kitchen. Seeing him, the man turns and points his camera at the detective who quickly raises his hand, striding forward, forcing the man back.

'You don't need my picture.'

In the kitchen, Chief Inspector Cattaneo, with his short-cropped hair and broad shoulders, stands, hands on hips, facing a table in the middle of the room. He turns in surprise.

'How did you get in here?'

'I came as soon as I heard,' says the detective, coming closer to the scene. At the table, the body of a man sits slumped at his breakfast. Bread and a *cuccuma* pot of coffee.

'Heard from whom?' says the inspector, only to wave his own question away with a swipe of his hand. The detective takes a Toscano cigar from his coat pocket and chews on the end of it.

The dead man is wearing nothing but a pair of creased cotton shorts. His long arms hang by his side, his knuckles touching the linoleum floor. A large chunk of bread protrudes from his mouth, stretched in an unnatural grimace. His dead eyes stare across the surface of the table at the pockmarked feasting of woodlice. Crumbs lie scattered around his head like a breaded nimbus in a depiction of some sainted peasant. Ciabatta loaves spill from a brown paper bag marked with the simple black ink emblem of a local bakery, *Il Panificio Levita*.

'So, what do you make of this?' asks the inspector.

From under his hat, the detective shoots a look at the man with the camera.

Cattaneo shakes his head. 'You done here, Inchiostro?'

The photographer removes his flat cap and rubs his prematurely balding head. He scans the room like he's checking whether he's missed anything important. His eyes keep shifting back to the bull of a man with the pinkish scar on his cheek, impatiently watching him.

'*Sì, fatto.*'

'*Va bene,*' says Cattaneo. 'Remember our deal.'

'Right,' says the photographer, backing out the room, like a crab in retreat. 'Discretion.'

The inspector crosses his arms and turns to the detective. 'Inchiostro's OK. We lack his technical skill at the department. In return he uses some of the pictures for the paper. Nothing shocking or too sensationalist.'

'Discretion, eh? Not sure that's a word the newspapers comprehend.'

'I understand your mistrust.'

'Do you?' says the detective, turning his attention back to the dead man. 'So, any ideas?'

'He choked to death. We know that much,' says the inspector.

The detective comes closer to the corpse: still a young man, late twenties, but barely any meat on his spindly arms and legs. Sporadic clusters of dark facial hair sprout from the sallow skin. Blood at the torn corners of the mouth. The loaf crushed in the middle.

'It's an execution,' he says. 'A warning.'

'*Beh*, he's well warned.'

'For others, I mean. The more violent the death, the more likely people are to remember.'

'You think your guy's responsible?'

The detective shifts his gait, crumbs crunching under his soles. He shakes his head. 'It's violent, but too messy.'

'But it's Mafia,' says the inspector. '*Maledetti.*'

'Perhaps. What do you know about the victim?'

'Tommaso Ciampa. Tommy or just Ciampa on the street. He's on our records. Arrests for theft and dealing in opium. He was an addict. I've taken him in a few times myself following raids on dens in this quarter. Right on his mother's doorstep. *Povera donna.* A widow. It's a miracle she gets by. Her son wasn't exactly a breadwinner.'

The detective raises his eyebrows.

'Sorry, you know what I mean.'

'Have you questioned her?'

'She's in shock. Didn't have much to say. Kept babbling on about her groceries. One of my men brought them up for her. He's asking her a few questions now. She'll be OK. She's of strong Sicilian stock. Probably seen worse.'

'That's perhaps why she's only talking about groceries.'

'That's your cynicism talking.'

He bites down on the cigar. 'Experience,' he says.

Two men in white coats arrive.

'We're here for the body,' says one of them, mistakenly addressing him, the officious looking man in overcoat and hat.

'We done?' asks the inspector.

The detective nods, tugging down his derby.

On the street, the inspector oversees the removal of the body. As the coroners' cart drives away, he rounds up his officers.

'I expect you'll let me know if you come up with anything.'

'Likewise,' says the detective, pocketing the cigar.

The inspector scowls. 'Why do you chew on those cheap cigars anyway?'

'They're no good for smoking.'

'Then why don't you get one you *can* smoke?'

'It doesn't agree with me. I quit.'

The inspector is about to say something else, but again he waves his question away. Then he and his men get into their automobile and head downtown.

The detective glances up at the apartment. At the window, the old woman stands looking out over the rooftops. The sun touches her face, and she closes her eyes, raising the backs of her hands to her cheeks. She remains basking in the sunlight, until the detective returns, ringing the bell to her apartment.

Three

With the late morning sunlight beaming through the window, covering the entire surface of the kitchen table with a shiny, ethereal cloth, the crime scene dissolves. The corpse no longer sits at the table. The offending loaves have been removed. But the police have been sloppy. Crumbs lie scattered on the floor. The old woman reaches for a dustpan and brush. She places her hand on the table for support as she tries to go down on her knees. But she stops and winces, placing a hand on her hip.

'Let me do that,' says the detective, taking the brush and pan from her.

'I've aches all over,' she says. 'A gift from old age.'

He gets down on his haunches and sweeps up the crumbs. His own back giving him trouble. He glances about the room. Not a cobweb in sight. He recalls his own mother's hours of housekeeping in their 5 cent tenement on Mulberry Street. As a bull, he'd visited the homes of other Italian immigrants living along the river on the Lower East Side, in the shadow of Brooklyn Bridge. The homes may have been poor, barely furnished, but they were always meticulously kept. Cleanliness is next to godliness, his mother used to say. But life in Lower Manhattan also taught him that even the most well-kept homes housed rats.

He is about to stand up when he notices a small, shiny object. Perhaps one of the widow's earrings. He fishes it out from the gap between the sink and the floorboards. A cufflink with the initials G.P. It appears to be real gold. He slips the cufflink into the pocket of his overcoat and gets slowly to his feet.

'Thank you,' says the widow.

'Signora – '

'Benedetta,' she says.

'*Sì*, Signora Benedetta, I understand it's difficult, but do you mind if I ask you a few more questions?'

'If it will help,' she says, glancing towards the window, at the sudden change of light.

He shifts his weight and takes from his pocket a notebook and pencil. 'What line of work was your son in?'

She lowers her head and clutches the key on the string around her neck, working it in her hand as though it were a rosary.

'Well, my Tommaso was like his father in that way.'

'You mean there was a family trade?'

'I wouldn't call it a trade. But they were both, let's say, entrepreneurial.'

'Business, then?'

'Tommaso, again like his father, tried his luck, but, well, not successfully.'

'Well, luck isn't for everybody.'

'I'd say we got more of the other sort,' she says, looking down at the chair.

'How about recently?'

She gazes at the ceiling and tilts her head to the side. 'Things were better. He'd become a kind of salesman.'

'Can you say what he was selling?'

'Oh no, he never told me things like that. Maybe magazines. Tommaso always did like his magazines.'

'Is there anything that you can remember about this morning? Something out of the ordinary, perhaps?'

She looks down at a white cup beside the *cuccuma* pot, its edges stained with coffee.

'There's one thing. I'm not sure it's important.'

'Yes?' he says, wetting the tip of the pencil with his tongue.

'Do you have a family, Signore?'

'I do,' he says, quietly.

'Then you understand how fussy family can be.'

'I'm not sure I follow.'

'Tommaso always sat in his chair, and I always sat in mine. He didn't like facing the sun, see?' She points to the window. 'And he always drank his coffee out of his cup. The blue porcelain, not this one.' She picks up the cup, turns it, frowning at the dirty rim, then quickly places it in the sink and washes her hands.

He presses the pencil down on the page.

'May I see his bedroom?'

She leads him back through the living room and hesitates before opening her son's door. The room is dark, and the air smells like an old sock full of gorgonzola. She feels her way

13

across the room and opens the shutters, then the window, letting in light and fresh air.

Although sparsely furnished with just a bed, side table, and a chair, the small room is a mess. Clothes lie strewn across the floor and draped over the back of the chair. The bed is unmade, and the linen looks damp and dirty.

'He didn't like me coming into his room,' she says.

The bedside table is littered with empty cigarette packets and matchboxes. Burnt matchsticks and strands of tobacco fill a cheap tin ashtray beside a folded newspaper and magazines, the kind that publish pictures of nude women. He covers them with the paper.

The widow busies herself picking up the soiled clothes from the chair and folding them distractedly. The detective places his hat beside him on the bed and discretely opens the bedside drawer. Beneath more magazines and sports almanacs lies an ornate, long-stemmed pipe decorated with elaborate carvings of poppies. He inspects the residue in the bulb with his fingertips. Opium. He pulls a handkerchief from his trouser pocket and wipes his hands. He puts the pipe back in the drawer, sweeps all the smut magazines inside too, and shuts it.

He stands up and paces. The widow frowns at his hat left on the bed, and he is quick to pick it up.

'Did your son ever have visitors, Signora Benedetta?'

She sighs, placing her hand on the neat pile of clothes. 'He wasn't the kind to bring friends home. Kept to himself mostly. He was a shy boy.' She falls silent and glances back towards the living room. 'There was a man who visited once,' she continues. 'His employer, I imagine. He always wore an expensive suit. Also, well, let's say *mangiava bene.*'

'You mean he was overweight?'

'I didn't want to say so, *ma sì.*'

'When was this?'

'Some weeks ago.'

'When he began working as a salesman?'

She nods. 'He'd become very diligent.'

He glances around the room. 'How so?'

'Well, he got up early for once. And he was out of the house more. Then, of course, there was breakfast.'

'Breakfast?'

'He didn't have much appetite before lunch, again like his father. Coffee in the morning, that's all. Until the bread deliveries started. I didn't understand what had come over him. But then I met, well, the man he worked for. *Hai capito?*'

'So, you think the bread was for his employer?'

'Who else, *se no?*'

'But you only met him the one time?'

'Just the once, *sì.* He didn't seem to like doing business with me around. But the bread was never eaten. And I didn't like the waste.'

'Never eaten, you say?'

'Don't worry, Signore. I would use the bread for the *trote.* Now that was a dish Tommaso liked. Deep fried in batter.' She touches her lips, then clutches the key around her neck. *'Alla fine, era un bravo ragazzo,'* she says. 'We all have bad habits, don't we, Signore?'

He nods, putting on his hat, forcing a smile.

Four

I t's an early start. The morning star still hangs bright beside a paling moon. In the light from the bakery window, the detective rubs his arms against the cold and attends to his cart and brushes. It didn't take much to convince the regular street sweep to rent him the small cart and wares of his trade. The old man seemed content with a day off and 5 lire for his trouble. Instead of his long overcoat and derby, he wears a workman's attire: white overalls, brown, stain-mottled boots, and a baggy flat cap, which shades his scar and dour peasant features. He is no stranger to assuming new identities. Going about in disguise amongst working-class Italians is what led to his promotion. Made lieutenant by Teddy Roosevelt himself. The first Italian to do so in the history of a police force dominated by Irishmen. Back in New York, it no longer irked him to be referred to as *the dago cop*. He wore that slur like a badge of honour. While here, he's just a *dago* amongst *dagos*.

He positions the cart at the corner wall adjacent to the bakery. He selects a hard brush, then crosses the street, and begins sweeping the gutters. It feels just like slipping into the old routine from his days as a whitewing, way back when the city street cleaners fell under the jurisdiction of the NYPD. He'd come far since then. Almost full circle.

A boy, no older than 17, wheels a bicycle out of the bakery. He is dressed in shorts and a short-sleeved collar shirt. His limbs are tanned and strong, statuesque, like a work by Michelangelo. The boy leans the bicycle against the shop window and adjusts the woven basket attached to the front. He checks the air pressure of the tyres. Then he removes a rag from his pocket and polishes the metal frame and white leather saddle. Afterwards, stuffing the rag in his back pocket, he steps away with his hands behind his back to admire his work.

A man wearing an apron marches out of the bakery, muttering and slapping the front page of a newspaper. The boy raises his hands and turns away and the man starts yelling in a recognizable dialect of the Campania region, one similar to his own. The boy snatches the paper and tosses it into the bin of the sweep's cart. The man lifts his hand, but he does not strike and the boy does not flinch. The scene is placated by a woman coming out with a flour sack filled with loaves individually wrapped in brown paper. She wears her hair beneath a sun orange headscarf. The man admonishes the boy with a hard look, but after a quick word from the woman he wipes his hands on his apron and returns inside.

The boy takes the bundle of bread and places it in the basket. The woman holds his face and kisses him on the forehead. A mother's kiss. When she has returned inside, the boy reaches for his bike but then pauses. He fishes the newspaper from the bin and reads. He lowers the paper and glances up and down the street, then, as though about to swat a fly, he rolls up the paper and throws it away again.

His mother comes out with a tin pail and rag to clean the windows. She seems surprised to see her son still there. But before she can speak, he takes his bicycle and carefully sets off, pedalling up the hill, his strong limbs making the task seem effortless.

Having cleaned the windows, the woman takes up the pail. She catches the sweep watching her. She gives him a reproachful look, but then she raises her hand and waves. He lifts his brush from the gutter and touches his cap.

As the first customers begin to queue, she goes back inside. He cleans the gutter to the end of the street.

When he's finished, he returns to the cart and retrieves the newspaper from the bin. On the front page of the *Milan Gazette* is the news of Tommaso Ciampa's death. While the article does not mention the bakery by name, in the corner of the photograph the bag of bread with the stamp of *Il Panificio Levita* is unmistakably there for all to see.

As the morning draws on, business is good. There is a steady flow of regular customers who greet the woman. The boy returns every half hour or so, and his mother is always quick to meet him. Her son gives her the empty sack, and she in turn hands him another, filled with fresh loaves. In the exchange, he notices the care with which the bundles are handled, carried as one might a pot of water that one fears spilling.

Around ten o'clock a tall, wiry man with a trim moustache walks up the street. He takes a seat at the single table outside Tullio's bar next door to the bakery. Almost immediately, a waiter brings the man an espresso and a glass of white wine. After taking a cigarillo from a silver case, he smokes and keeps his eyes on the entrance to the bakery.

When there are no customers, the woman comes outside. Seeing the man at the table, she frowns. They seem to know each other, but there is no warmth in their greetings. He raises his wine and sips. With a brief nod, she turns and wastes no time returning inside.

The sweep takes up his broom and moves closer to the bar. He notices the man's gold ring, his fine tailored suit and polished oxfords, worn by some of the less discreet *capos* back in New York. When he is close enough to the man's table, he sighs heavily.

'*Fa caldo, vero?*' he says. *Hot, isn't it?*

With his eyes always on the bakery, the man replies in a strong Sicilian accent, '*Sì, fa caldo.*'

'Where in the Old Country are you from?' says the sweep.

'*Un paesino,*' says the man. *A small village.*

It's the guarded language typical of a *mafioso*, saying something but giving away nothing.

'*Ho capito,*' says the sweep.

'*Buon lavoro,*' the Sicilian says, reaching for his wine and effectively ending their conversation.

The sweep moves off, back to his cart.

When the boy returns at midday his mother receives the sack, but there is no more bread for him to deliver. His work is done.

The Sicilian calls the boy. He hesitates, and his mother stares hard at the man. He waves her away, a gesture that says, 'get on with it', and she goes inside, clasping the back of her neck.

The Sicilian says something to the boy, which he cannot make out. The boy understands and looks at his bicycle and shakes his head. The Sicilian raises his hands in resignation, then takes a banknote from his pocket and, with the note tightly folded between his fingers, holds it out to the boy. He refuses the note, but the Sicilian insists with rough words. The boy is about to take the money when his mother returns and, in her stern dialect, tells him to take his bicycle inside. He obeys. Again, while holding the door open for her son, the woman glowers at the Sicilian.

The man finishes his wine, then, slipping a few lire notes under his glass, he stands and leaves. The waiter is quick to appear, to clear away, and take the money. He doesn't count it. It is more than enough.

The sweep and the woman watch on as the Sicilian disappears down the street. When the tall man is gone, her eyes turn to him. She tries to smile and half waves, but it seems to take tremendous effort, and she retreats inside the shop.

Five

At midday, the sweep dusts himself off and enters Finn's Bar. The Irishman scratches his red beard as he looks up from a newspaper.

'Well, look who it is?' he says with a roguish smile. 'What's with the overalls, Velletri?'

'New job,' he says, taking a seat and slapping his baggy cap on the stool beside him.

'What? You cleaning windows?'

'Something like that.'

'How about a beer? Can't be fun out in this heat.'

'Just a glass of chianti,' he says, glancing at Finn's paper.

'Help yourself,' he says. 'I'm done.'

The detective scans the front page of the *New York Herald*. Finn's bar is the only place he knows of where he can read the news from home. Most of the Irishman's customers are expats. Finn himself sailed over on the *Duca di Genova* years ago. New Yorkers never leave the city for good. They're always looking back.

Reading the Italian press and the *Herald*, the detective has followed the investigation of the Palermo police closely for months. While the details differ, one fact remains the same:

the investigation has reached a dead end. As usual, the Dons have succeeded in bribing the officials. Of course, he knows who did the shooting. He was there.

'Anything I should worry about?' says Finn, serving the glass of chianti with a small ramekin of olives.

'You should try reading more than the sports pages, Finn.'

'Then we'd have nothing to talk about,' he says, grinning.

The detective sighs. The *New York Herald*, the paper responsible for both his legacy and his undoing. The tributes to him are no longer printed. He's been forgotten. New stories have pushed him from the front pages. New heroes, but the same breed of villain. He takes a sip of wine and turns to the cultural pages to see what's showing on Broadway.

Finn leans across the bar. 'Why worry about Broadway when you have La Scala?'

He shrugs. 'Broadway is Broadway.'

'Come on, Velletri. You can't compare those sing-a-longs to the works of Verdi or Puccini.'

'What do you know about it?' says Ofelia, coming out of the kitchen.

'More than you, I bet,' Finn says, smiling at his wife.

Her good-natured face and long, dark curls make her the raven-haired sister of Botticelli's Venus.

'Good to see you, Giuseppe,' she says, drying her hands on a dishrag. 'New job?'

'Street sweep,' he says, folding the paper. 'Pays the rent.'

'And doesn't he clean up nicely, *cara*?'

'Ignore him,' she says. 'How about some lunch? I've got some fresh olive focaccia from the new bakery.'

So, he thinks, *Il Panificio Levita*. The talk of the town. He's curious to know what all the fuss is about. He orders a plate of Asiago and Parmigiana cheese along with the focaccia. Ofelia hurries off to the kitchen.

'Always happy to please,' says Finn, watching her go.

'She's a good catch,' he says.

The Irishman's eyes soften, gazing at the kitchen door as if he's suddenly in love with it. The detective sips his wine and smiles. Listening to the hotwire back-and-forth of English and Italian is what he likes most about his visits to Finn and Ofelia. He feels right at home.

'What do you know about the family?' he asks Finn.

'*La famiglia* Levita? Not much,' he says, snapping out of his reverie. 'It's just the baker, his wife, and their son. They set up a few weeks back. We used to buy our bread from the market, but then Davide came in one day to introduce himself and – '

'Davide?'

'That's the baker's son,' says Ofelia, returning with the food.

'And that's when he stole the business from the poor *ragazzi* at the market,' says Finn.

'He didn't steal anything,' she says. 'He just offered a really good service.'

'Bread delivery,' says Finn. 'Never heard such a crazy idea.'

'It's great,' says Ofelia. 'It saves me a lot of time.'

'And he delivers it every day?' says the detective.

'Fresh as you like,' she says.

'By bicycle,' says Finn. 'Wonder what else he's peddling.'

'*Ma taci tu*,' she says, raising a fist. 'And we only have to pay at the end of the week.'

'Pay more at that,' says Finn, scratching his beard.

'It's better bread,' she says.

'The boy's very cunning for his age, I'll say that. If I had half the street smarts he has, I'd be rich or in jail.'

'*Basta*,' she says, walloping him with the dishrag. 'It's not street anything. It's hard, honest work, something you haven't quite grasped. Anyway, the service saves me a lot of hassle, and the customers love it.'

The detective takes a bite of the focaccia. The crust is crisp, the inside, *soffice*, just the way his own *nonna* used to make it. He takes another big bite and washes it down with a gulp of chianti.

Six

In the late afternoon, he makes his way back down Via Paolo Sarpi to his post outside the bakery. On a corner, a group of four boys, rough types who should be in school, crowd around a young dog, a retriever crossbreed, one of the many mongrels that roam the quarter. The smallest of the boys holds the dog by the scruff of its neck while another attaches what looks like a makeshift collar of string and twigs. The dog yelps and cowers close to the ground. It's only when one of the older boys takes out a box of matches that the detective realises what these young hoodlums are up to. He's about to shout out, when the baker's son appears on his bicycle, racing past him, down the street. He brakes suddenly beside the boys.

'*Ma che state facendo?*' he says, letting his bike fall. *What are you doing?*

He grabs the boy with the matches by the wrist just as he is about to light the *petardi* strung around the whimpering dog's neck.

'*Lasciami stare.*' *Let go.* Using his elbows, the boy fights back, but Davide knocks him to the ground with the force of his knee.

An older boy stands up and shoves Davide in the chest.

'*Fai i cazzi tuoi, terrone,*' he says. *Mind your own fucking business, southerner.*

Then, while the youngest is left holding the dog, the others get to their feet. Davide is outnumbered. But he is quick, hitting the oldest and strongest first in the gut with his fist and then, as the big kid doubles over, with another blow across the cheek. The other boys back up, giving Davide some room, only for a wiry kid to bring a stick down on his back. The blow only serves to provoke the baker's son's temper, and before the kid can strike again Davide snatches the stick from him and lashes out with a fierce kick. The kid drops to the ground in a heap clutching his balls. Wielding the stick in front of him like a baseball bat, Davide faces the others who have moved further back, taunting him with names, while being sure to stay out of his reach. The small boy left holding the dog looks up at him.

'*Togli quella cosa,*' says Davide. *Take that thing off.*

The young boy gazes at the dog and caresses its fur as it covers its snout with its paws. Then, despite being yelled at by the others, the boy removes the collar from around the animal's neck. Freed from the kid's grasp, the mongrel bolts across the street and hides beneath a hedge. More like a cat in retreat than a dog.

'*Dammela,*' says Davide, reaching out a hand. *Give it to me.*

'*Ma non è mia,*' says the boy, looking at the older kid nursing his cheek. *But it isn't mine.*

'*Me ne frego.*' *I don't care.* Davide takes a step forward, but the boy drops the collar to the ground and runs.

Hearing the racket, a shopkeeper comes out of his store threatening to call the police. The boys are quick to move off. Davide, too. Throwing the stick aside, he picks up his bicycle and checks it for any damage. Then, seeming satisfied, he saddles his bike and rides away.

The detective continues down the street. Coming to the abandoned collar, he crushes it underfoot, then sweeps it up and tosses it in the bin. Across the way, the dog has emerged from its hiding place and, with its tail wagging, it trots off, in the direction of the bakery.

Setting his cart outside the shop window, he sees the retriever lying vigilant at the door, a bowl of water nearby. The sweep adjusts his baggy cap and enters the bakery. There are only a few customers. In the corner, beside his bicycle, Davide sits on a stool. On the wall hangs a framed picture of Saint Gennaro, the patron saint of Naples. The boy takes from his breast pocket a picture postcard: a print of a photograph perhaps, a portrait of some kind. He studies it with his eyes bright, a slight smile on his lips, and hums the tune of Donizetti's *Te voglio bene assaie*. He appears unaffected by the fight with the boys only moments ago. If anything, he seems content with the world.

Behind the counter, Davide's mother serves another customer. She is wearing glasses, and her hair is wound neatly in a bun. She jots down the sale in a ledger beside the cash register, then she slips her short pencil behind her ear.

'*Prego*, can I help you?' she says.

He doffs his cap, and she recognises him. She smiles, removing her glasses.

'You're working hard,' she says. 'You've been out there since this morning.'

'I'm new here,' he says in his dialect.

The boy falls silent and glances curiously at the stranger. Then he returns his attention to the picture and picks up humming again. The Donizetti tune appears stuck on the chorus.

'Well, what can I offer you?' says the boy's mother. 'We don't have much left.'

But for a few loaves, the baskets behind her are empty. Beneath the baskets, on trays, are *struffoli, roccocò, susamielli,* and other treats typical of the *pasticcerie* in Campania.

'For now, I just need directions, *per favore*?'

The boy raises an eyebrow and tucks the picture back in his pocket.

'We're new to the neighbourhood ourselves,' she says. 'But I'll do my best.'

'I need to get to La Scala.'

'Going to a show?'

'Oh no. I have another job to do before this evening.'

At the door to the kitchen, the baker appears. His black hair is streaked with white. It is difficult to tell whether it's marked by age or simply dusted with flour. Wiping his hands on his apron, he greets the sweep with a brusque, *'Buona sera.'*

'La Scala?' she says, looking at her husband.

'It's a long way from here,' says the baker, putting his hands into a pocket in the front of his apron. 'But the tram will get you there quick enough.'

'Oh no,' the sweep says, pointing out the window to his cart, 'you see?'

The woman waves her husband away, but he stays put.

'Davide,' says the baker, 'stop humming. We can't hear ourselves think.'

Without looking at his father, the boy falls silent and, gazing at the dog at the door, plays with his bottom lip.

'*Senta*,' she says, 'I think I can help you. If you make your way to Parco Sempione, then go straight down Via Dante, which becomes Via Orefici, I think…. Anyway, at the end of it, you'll see the Duomo, and, well, La Scala is only about a block or two away.'

'*Ma no, mamma*,' says the boy, getting up from his stool. 'There's an easier way.' He looks at the stranger earnestly. '*Senta Signore*, simply continue down Via Bramante, cross Piazzale Biancamano, head towards Via Solferini, then go straight down until Via Brera which becomes Via Giuseppe Verdi. That'll lead you directly to La Scala. *Si fa presto.*'

The woman smiles at her son. 'There you have it,' she says.

'*Grazie*,' says the sweep. 'You sure know your way around.'

The boy shrugs and smiles. His father again wipes his hands on his apron and returns to the kitchen.

'That's a fine bicycle,' he says.

The boy slaps the white saddle and rings the bell. At the entrance, the dog lifts its head and barks.

'I keep it inside the store when I am not delivering.'

'Thieves,' says his mother, reaching for the pencil behind her ear.

'I see you're a strong bicyclist,' says the sweep.

The boy smiles, gripping the handlebars as though he were about to give a demonstration of his talents right there in the shop.

'Davide wants to win the Giro d'Italia,' says his mother.

'The race starts right here in Milan,' says the boy.

'He even met this year's winner, didn't you Davide?'

The boy nods and takes the picture from his pocket and shows it to the sweep. A handsome rider with a moustache and the thighs of a giant poses on a racing bike with the hills of Lombardy in the background. It is signed, *Luigi Ganna. Campione del primo Giro d'Italia, 1909*. The boy gazes at it again before slipping it away safely.

The baker returns. 'Can we do anything else for you, Signore? Some bread, perhaps?'

Both the boy and his mother glare at the baker. He crosses his arms.

'*Per favore*,' says the woman, 'try some of these. My husband's speciality.'

She fills one of the brown paper bags with *roccocò*. The baker disappears into the kitchen. The clanging of an oven door, a crashing of trays follow.

'*Ecco*,' she says. 'It's a reward, for your hard work.'

'*Grazie mille*,' he says, taking the bag from her.

'I'm Edda, and this is Davide.' She gives a cautionary glance to the kitchen. 'My husband's name is Jacopo.'

'*Piacere*,' says the sweep, doffing his cap. '*Mi chiamo* Simone Saulino.'

Outside, he bites into one of the *roccocò* and sighs. The retriever peers up at him, yawns, and licks its jowls. He wags his finger at the dog, then takes up his cart and pushes it back up the hill.

So, now he's *Simone Saulino*. Why had he gone and used Adelina's maiden name? It came to him instantly, falling off his tongue, a lie more easily uttered than the truth. He recalls his time aboard the *Duca di Genova*, where, for the most part, he'd stuck to his assumed name, in which his ticket had been issued. But there'd been occasions, conversing to fellow passengers, when he'd inexplicably introduced himself as Guglielmo Simone. Guglielmo? *Dio, perché?*

Further along, a group of children play football in the street. Back home around the Lower East Side, kids their age would have greeted him respectfully, or even invited him to play a game of baseball. But here now, he is just a street sweep. They don't even know his name. Nobody does. Soon even he will forget who he really is. He drops the *roccocò* in the bag and pulls his cap low over his eyes.

Seven

C loser to home, he plods through the busy alley. Despite the late hour the heat of the day has not abated and neither has the activity. Women chat above the whirr of their sewing machines and the whip-whop of their looms. He returns the cart to the makeshift shed beneath the apartment of the old man, the regular sweep who sits in a vest on his balcony overgrown with ivy, fanning himself with a large ornate paper fan, like an impoverished emperor abandoned by his concubines. The detective waves.

'*A domani?*' says the man, hopeful of another 5 lire.

'*Si, a domani,*' he says, ducking beneath the hanging sheets and other bed linen that are only taken in after sundown.

The lobby of the *pensione* is empty at this time. The proprietor, Madam Xuan, conducts her business in the morning. The sound of Chinese opera coming from her rooms in the early evening is a warning that she is not to be disturbed. Not even the young maid Yang, with her soft slippered feet, padding about as quiet as a mouse, can be heard.

As far as he can tell, Madam Xuan manages more than the *pensione* in Chinatown. Not only overseeing the flower market but controlling deals in the textile industry, too. Business owners wait each morning to receive her council. These dangerous looking men seem to respect, if not fear her.

When business is done, Madam Xuan appears equally in her element arranging flowers in the vases that decorate the ground floor. Sometimes it looks more like a church at *Pasqua* than the lobby to a boarding house.

The door to her rooms is open. The snip of pruning scissors and her singing keep him fixed at the foot of the staircase. He waits, his hand poised on the banister, and listens. All sense of urgency is lost. He learnt all too late that there are moments that occur only once, and if they are not held onto, there and then, they will be lost, never to return again. Small gifts that one should not refuse, lest they be the last.

She stops singing. The soft sweep of her gown crosses the wooden floor. Before he can escape up the stairs, she is at the door.

'Is there something you need, Signor Joe?'

She leans against the doorframe, her long black hair in a wave across her left shoulder, down to the belt that fastens her red silk nightgown. She smokes a long-stemmed cigarette. A Parisian brand he knows costs the earth. In her other hand, she holds the pair of scissors. The blades pointing down.

'No,' he says, backstepping. 'I was just wondering – '

'Yes, Signor Joe?'

He likes that she calls him Joe, but it makes him nervous.

'Did any letters arrive for me?' he asks.

'Are you expecting letters?'

'No,' he says.

'Then none came.' Her mouth quivers as if she is about to give away a smile. Instead, she expels a plume of smoke and turns suddenly, going back into her rooms, the end of her gown trailing like a tail.

She is gone before he thinks to speak again.

'*Grazie*,' he says, looking down at his boots, then plods up the stairs to his room.

Through the lattice curtains, the last of the day's sunlight paints floral patterns on the dressing table. He sets down his notebook, pencil, and a few lire coins. He eases off his boots, slips his revolver beneath his pillow, and removes his overalls. In his boxer shorts and white vest, he slumps heavily on the edge of the bed. *Is there something you need, Signor Joe?*

Back home only his closest friends and…. Well, only a few people called him Joe. On arriving at the *pensione* back in June, just off the night train from Lecce, still groggy from the morphine that had been his staple diet since his retreat from Palermo, he'd not had the presence of mind to use the name now on his passport. Madam Xuan had opened the register and handed him a fountain pen. He'd clutched it clumsily and signed his name, Giuseppe Velletri. She'd pressed her thumb to his signature and said, 'thank you, Signor Joe,' as if somehow she knew. To avoid suspicion, he's remained so. Besides, he finds some solace in it being partly true. In being partly himself.

The towel he used to cover the mirror has fallen. He didn't think himself a vain man. But he supposes vanity is an instinct for survival. Without it, people would give in to death much sooner.

In the patterned sunlight, his scars are pink against his pale skin. Right shoulder, neck, cheek. He touches each of his wounds in turn, as if warding off *malocchio*. To conclude this ritual, he places his hand flat on his chest. Where the fourth bullet had hit. But the bluish ink-like bruise has healed, and there is no scar.

He opens the drawer. A picture postcard of the Duomo di Monreale, his pocket watch, and his NYPD police badge, number 285. He pushes the badge to the back of the drawer and picks up the watch. He presses his thumb into the bullet dent, then opens the cap. The hands stopped on 8:50. There'd been no need for a coroner to determine the time of death. To think that he once doubted the watch was real gold. He shuts the cap, kisses the watch, places it back in the drawer beside the postcard. He is tempted to read it but knows what will follow. Instead, he closes his eyes and says a silent prayer. *Che Dio li protegga.* He shuts the drawer and collapses on the bed.

Hazy yellow light from weak gas lamps lights the deserted piazza. Cobblestones rise from puddles, like boiled eggs in a muddy broth. The distant bell of a streetcar and the murmur of passengers, huddled against the cold, waiting to depart. A garden of exotic plants looms high, hedged in by an iron fence. As he turns, his back to the fence, three figures emerge from the shadow of the church. The gas lamps give out, and darkness falls before they can reach him. Four pistol shots – three at once, then a single shot, rupture the silence of the piazza.

Eight

A rapid series of hard knocks pummel his door like machine-gun fire. He leaps up, grabbing his .38 from under his pillow.

'Signor Velletri, wake up,' says Chupeng.

The detective drags a hand down his face and pushes himself up from the bed. Hiding the gun behind his back, he slowly opens the door. The street kid stands in the hall in the light of a lantern held by Madam Xuan. Her hair is plaited into a single cord, which she strokes gently, as though it were her pet.

'Come quick,' says Chupeng.

'What time is it? Come where?'

'Murder, Signor Velletri.'

Madam Xuan studies his expression, then lowers her eyes.

The otherwise quiet streets of Chinatown are pierced by the screeching of cats out for a fight. He follows the boy who darts quick as a rabbit down the alleys. On Via Monte Asolone, a narrow street not far from the cemetery, two police officers stand guard at the entrance to a rundown municipal housing block. By the time the detective crosses the road, Chupeng has vanished into the night, like some fairy-tale imp.

One of the policemen, judging by the stripes on his shoulder mark and stiff lampshade moustache, is a high-ranking officer, while the other appears to be a recruit. The officer shoots the detective a hard look.

Lowering his hat, he asks for Chief Inspector Cattaneo.

The recruit, giving him the benefit of the doubt, goes inside the building, while the officer blocks the way with one arm outstretched and a hand ready on his gun belt.

Soon Cattaneo emerges from the dark hallway. The light from a streetlamp strikes down, and the inspector squints, shading his eyes with his hand.

'*Ancora tu?*' he says, brushing his hand back over his short-cropped hair. *You again.* Then he shrugs and gestures for the detective to follow him. The officer does not make way, and so he shoulders past, feeling his pulse surge.

The ground floor apartment is filthy, looking like it's been lived in by more than just the poor, dead soul lying face down, arms out in front, over a low coffee table in a mess of blood and playing cards. The victim is on his knees beside a cushion. More cushions surround the table. Crouched across from the body, the young fellow with the flat cap resets his flash. He gives the detective a nod, then snaps a shot of the corpse.

'Two shots were fired,' says Cattaneo. 'The first hit the cabinet over there, and the second was fatal. Well, eventually. He bled to death. *Povero bastardo.*'

The detective puts on a pair of brown leather gloves and gets down on his haunches beside the body. Watching with interest, the photographer pulls his cap from his shiny bald head and dabs his brow with his forearm. Then he leans in with his camera, causing the detective to growl.

'Inchiostro,' says Cattaneo, snapping his fingers. 'I'd say it's past your bedtime.'

The photographer nods and, back stepping out the door, tips his cap to the detective and, it seems, to the dead man.

The detective examines the entry wound at the base of the man's throat. 'Judging by the amount of powder burn, my guess is a revolver, possibly a Bodeo.'

'From the Old Country?'

'Can't say,' he says.

'I'm asking if you think it's your Sicilian friend, this Don?'

The detective shakes his head, frowning at the word *friend*. 'The Don seldom does his own killing. Anyway, there's no *colpo di grazia,* the signature of any respectable assassin. No, whoever's responsible for this mess probably never fired a gun before.'

The inspector nods, examining the hole in the panel of the cabinet.

'The body was moved,' says the detective.

'How do you figure? He was shot from the front and fell forward.'

'Right, but if you look at his position, it isn't natural. This cushion was pulled out from under him after he was shot. He was probably hiding something, *denaro*, maybe.' He searches amongst the cushions and fishes out some playing cards, a pair of aces, and a long-stemmed pipe. He sniffs the bulb and passes it to the inspector.

'Opium,' says Cattaneo. 'That's no surprise. The man's name is Francesco Crippa, or Franky to the girls who worked for him. Previous arrests for pimping, extortion, dealing. And clearly also a cheat at poker. *Che pasticcio.*'

Searching the man's pockets, the detective finds a slip of paper torn from a brown paper bag. Written in pencil is the amount of 500 lire.

'What are you doing there now?' says the inspector, growing irritated. 'The forensics boys still need to have a look around, and you've already put your paws into everything. Anyway, how is it you keep showing up like this?'

The detective shrugs. 'I live in the neighbourhood.'

Cattaneo drags a hand over his haggard features. 'You need to remember this is Milan police business. Unlike you, I'm here to protect the citizens of this city. I won't pretend you haven't been through hell, but that doesn't make Milan open hunting ground for your crusade, or a vendetta, if that's what this is, *hai capito?*'

Slipping the piece of paper into his coat, the detective gets slowly to his feet. '*Ho capito,*' he says, removing his gloves.

Having left the crime scene and the inspector's foul mood behind, he walks back down Via Monviso. He toys with the scrap of paper in his pocket. How are the Levita family involved in this mess? 500 lire is a lot of bread.

About to turn down his street, he hears footsteps behind him and turns quickly. In the near dark, he makes out the figure of a man tailing him. He proceeds to the next corner and presses his body up against a store window, concealing himself in the shadows of the awning. He pulls the .38 from under his overcoat. The man walks slowly past, appears to sense something amiss, and stops.

Cocking his gun, the detective steps out of the shadows.

The man turns in surprise. 'Wait,' he says, removing his flat cap. In the dark, his shiny head glows like a moon. 'I just want to talk.'

'You're that photographer,' he says, lowering his gun.

'*Sì,* my name's Alvise Inchiostro.'

'Inchiostro, that's right. What are you doing following me? I've killed men for less.'

'*Giusto*' he says, tentatively putting on his cap. 'I thought maybe we could help each other.'

'I don't think so.' He slips his gun back beneath his coat.

'Back at the apartment you mentioned the Mafia.'

'You were snooping?'

'I was investigating,' he says. 'I'm not just a photographer, you know. It's called investigative journalism.'

'Thanks for the schooling, *ragazzo*.'

'We're on the same side, you and I.'

'How's that?'

'You seem to be police, but you're not like any police 'round here.'

'I'm not police,' he says. '*Buona notte.*' He walks on.

'I know about Don Vito,' he says. 'I can help you.'

The detective stops and turns. 'What do you know?'

'I know that he has operations right across the north, many here in Milan.'

'So, how's that news to me?'

41

'I've pictures of the men who work for him. That's what you want, isn't it? Whoever you are. If you find them, you find Don Vito, right?'

'How do I know I can trust you? You could be one of their stoolies?'

'What's a stoolie?'

'A spy, a rat. Spilling what you know for money.'

'I'm a respectable journalist.'

He laughs. 'Respectable? Do you know what Don Vito loves more than money, more than power?'

Inchiostro shakes his head.

'Respect,' he says.

'*Senta*, how about you read some of my articles,' says the journalist, reaching into his jacket pocket. 'Here's my card. If you change your mind, call me. I want to see Don Vito put away as much as you do.'

The detective slips the card into his pocket. 'Why?'

'Why?'

'Why are you so interested in Don Vito?'

'The same reason you are. People here live in fear of the Sicilian Mafia, the Camorra clans, the 'Ndrangheta, and there are others. People are afraid to speak up. My job is to speak for them. If someone speaks, then hopefully there'll be someone who listens, and acts.'

The detective touches the brim of his derby. 'Fair enough,' he says. 'As long as you know that speaking can get you killed.'

'I know,' he says.

'See you, Signor Inchiostro.' The detective walks away.

'Wait, what do I call you?'

'You don't,' he says without looking back, 'I'll call you.'

'Your name, I mean?'

The detective stops and scratches the back of his neck. 'Velletri,' he says, glancing back at the journalist. 'You can call me Giuseppe Velletri.'

Nine

As the sun rises, a dark red hue seeps through the gaps between the buildings, flooding the streets. With cart, brushes, and dressed in his sweep's attire, he returns to the bakery. He secures the cart to the post of a streetlamp and waits beneath the awning of the barbershop.

The light in the bakery is on, but the blinds are drawn. There is no sign of Davide or his bicycle. The first early morning customers stand outside. Behind the blinds, the silhouetted figures of the Levita couple shift about. A few men pull out their pocket watches. Women try to peer through the window. An incensed old lady eventually raps at the door.

Edda raises the blinds and opens up. She apologises, inviting the customers in, and goes behind the counter. The people crowd quickly into the small bakery, as if the bread were not enough to go around. With his baggy cap pulled low, he hangs back attentively behind the throng.

Edda looks as if she has aged overnight. While her hair is thrust up and hidden beneath an azure headscarf, wild strands escape against her cheek. Her face is pale, her eyes are puffy beneath her glasses.

The ill-tempered old woman is now the most cheerful, talking loudly and asking after the Levita family's health. 'Where is your handsome son?' she croons.

Edda appears not to hear anything the woman says and goes about her work, while her eyes dart constantly to the window. Then, recognising the sweep, her eyes soften and her bottom lip trembles slightly. The next customer asks for a half dozen loaves, and Edda regains herself, attempting a smile.

He goes back outside and peers up and down Via Paolo Sarpi. Just then, the wiry Sicilian with the moustache comes striding up the street. Lagging behind him, a short, robust kid pushes a bicycle fitted with a woven basket, the saddle bright white. Davide's bicycle. As they draw up to the shop, the kid begins ringing the mechanical bell, until the Sicilian rebukes him with a raised fist.

They chat quietly amongst themselves, taking no notice of the sweep. The kid takes a pack of cigarettes from his back pocket and pops one between his fat cherub lips. When the Sicilian goes into the shop, the detective follows.

On seeing the man, Edda calls her husband. The other customers, wary of the tall, well-dressed figure, fall silent. Even the garrulous old woman, who has just received her bread, bundles her purchases into her grocery bag and leaves quickly without another word.

The baker hurries out the kitchen. The remaining customers make way, some head for the door. The sweep moves into the corner, beneath the picture of Saint Gennaro, who appears now to be looking up to heaven in dismay.

'Where's our son?' says the baker, his voice strained.

The Sicilian does not answer. Instead, he calmly lights a cigarillo, draws in deeply, then expels pungent smoke that wafts through the aroma of warm bread.

The baker rushes forward and grabs the Sicilian by the lapels of his tan linen jacket.

'Where is Davide? *Dimmelo.*' He drives the Sicilian back out of the shop. Edda dashes after them. The sweep follows, along with the rest of the customers, and he stands amongst them and other curious passers-by. The robust kid, leaning against the wall smoking, watches the scene with interest. Edda sees her son's bicycle and, pulling the headscarf from her hair, she searches up and down the street, calling out.

'Davide?'

With his forehead thrust against the tall man's chin, the baker pushes the Sicilian back to the edge of the sidewalk. The kid flicks away his cigarette and steps forward, pulling out a knife. The sweep waits, ready, gripping his revolver in the pocket of his overalls. Not wanting to intervene unless he has to.

The Sicilian, the cigarillo dangling from his lips, calmly takes the baker by the wrists. '*Sta calmo,*' he says.

The baker lunges for the man's throat. But the Sicilian is fast. Sidestepping, he hits the baker with a swift backhand that knocks him stumbling to the ground. The kid follows up with a kick and is about to use his knife, when the Sicilian warns him off, '*Basta.*' The kid obeys with a sulky glare at the bleeding baker who nurses his face where a cut has opened above his eye. Edda runs to her husband.

'*Vi prego*, Rizzo, *basta*.'

She wipes the blood from Jacopo's face with her scarf.

The Sicilian drops the cigarillo into the gutter and adjusts the gold ring on his finger.

'If your husband wasn't such a *testa calda*, you'd know the good news already,' he says, brushing flour here and there from his jacket.

'The good news?' says Jacopo, rising slowly to his feet with Edda's help.

'Your son is doing more important work. This here is Bonifacio.'

The kid smiles and slips the knife back into his pocket.

'He will deliver your bread from now on.'

All eyes turn to Davide's bicycle against the wall. The kid spits into the street.

'*Non è possibile –* ' begins the baker, but his wife touches her fingertips to his lips.

'*Lascia fare a me*,' she says, her voice measured but firm. 'What is our son doing?'

'You shouldn't worry,' says the Sicilian. 'He has a job, that's good, no? In the meantime, I suggest you all get on with your own.' He glances at the kid who raises his hands innocently.

The baker, ready to fight another round, is hushed back into the shop by Edda. She attends to her hair, hanging dishevelled about her face, and, with her bloodied headscarf in her fist, follows her husband. The Sicilian calls the kid over and appears to give him instructions.

Soon Edda comes out with the sack of wrapped loaves and the kid takes them roughly.

'You took your time,' he says. 'You'd better be ready when I come back.'

She holds her tongue but looks to the Sicilian to intervene. 'When will Davide be home?' she says.

But the Sicilian shrugs and says nothing.

New customers enter the shop. Edda drops her head and goes inside. The Sicilian walks back down the street, lighting up another cigarillo. The sweep, his baggy cap pulled down just above his eyes, follows at a distance.

Ten

The Sicilian cuts his way through the streets of China-town. He smokes as he walks. His tall, wiry build expels the attitude of a dangerous man. Like a snake slipping through the short grass, he is recognised for who he is and what he might do. Chinese storekeepers avoid making eye contact when he passes. If you don't see the devil, he doesn't see you. Then they watch as he goes on, relieved that they have escaped a brush with Death.

Occasionally the man will stop at a store to collect or have a quiet word. But mostly he watches, sitting at cafés where he always orders an espresso and glass of white wine. A combination which appears to keep his mood in balance. If he is greeted, it is with respect, or fear, as if he wore a hooded robe and carried a sickle. Or does the figure of Death appear differently to the Chinese?

At midday, at yet another café, the Sicilian checks his pocket watch. He finishes his wine, drops a wad of notes on the table, and leaves. The waiter makes sure the tall man is gone before clearing up and gathering the loot.

The Sicilian hops on a tram outside Stazione Centrale. The detective is quick to catch the same one, staying out of sight, hiding as best he can amongst the other passengers returning home for *l'ora di pranzo*.

He almost loses the Sicilian when he unexpectedly jumps off the tram and moves, as quick as a lizard, through the streets towards the Duomo. He is a typical specimen of the Mafia: if you cut off its tail, it soon grows a new one.

Arriving in Piazza del Duomo, the Sicilian walks up to the cathedral and drops a coin into the tin cup of a raggedy beggar at the door, then goes inside.

At this hour, the church will be empty, and the detective risks being seen. He takes his chances and goes in. Standing at the entrance, behind one of the stone columns, he removes his cap. The Sicilian kneels at a pew in the front of the altar and bows his head. The detective has met many men like him. Men who can inflict suffering with one hand and ask forgiveness with the other. It's a case of not letting your left hand know what the right is doing. That may not be how priests see it. But there are other men, men on opposite sides of the Law, who interpret God's law in the same way. He himself is one of those men.

The opulence of the cathedral depresses him. He decides to wait outside. He buys the *Milan Gazette* at a nearby kiosk and waits at a safe distance. Soon the Sicilian leaves, ignoring the beggar who once again raises his tin for alms. The detective folds his paper and continues his pursuit.

It ends in a well-to-do residential area not far from La Scala. On Via dei Lussi, the Sicilian disappears inside a two-storied villa with a front garden. Cypress trees line both sides of the street, offering the detective cover, but he still feels conspicuous. He sits on a bench far enough from the house to go unnoticed, but close enough to observe. Opening the newspaper, he waits and watches.

The villa is guarded by a large, muscular man who bides his time pruning the rose bushes in the garden. He seems more suited for the part of a strongman in a circus than as a gardener. Men come and go from the house. Whenever they approach, the gardener leaves his roses to meet them at the steps. If he knows them to be friends, so called men of respect, he will simply nod as they pass inside. However, if they are men who have come to pay their dues, he will search them before allowing them to be escorted by a second man into the house.

An hour passes before Davide appears, coming outside to chat with the gardener. Taking the buds gently in hand, he seems to discuss his roses with Davide who is content to listen. Their conversation is interrupted when a pair of French doors open on the balcony, and an overweight man in a pinstriped suit steps out. He tells Davide to come upstairs. The gardener shrugs and pats Davide on the back.

On returning into the house, the boy stops, turns, and looks directly at the detective. He raises the paper and pretends to read. When he looks up again, Davide is up on the balcony with the fat man. He caresses Davide's cheek. The boy turns his head away, but the man rebukes him, grabbing him by a tuft of hair. Davide, with his shoulders hunched, goes inside, and the fat man follows him, shutting the French doors behind him.

It is early evening when the detective returns to the bakery. There is no sign of the kid Bonifacio. Attending to a few customers, Edda glances the detective's way. She doesn't seem surprised to see him. He bides his time, and when the last customer leaves, he shuts the door and locks it.

'Signor Saulino?' Edda says, slowly closing the ledger.

'*Sentite*, I can help you.'

She slips her pencil behind her ear. 'Jacopo,' she says.

The baker comes out. His eye is swollen, and the cut is stained with yellow ointment.

'You again,' he says. 'What do you want?'

'He says he can help us,' says Edda.

'How?' he says, glaring at the detective. 'And why are we closed? We must continue business. They'll hear about this.' He marches towards the door, but his wife steps in front of him.

'Wait,' she says, facing the sweep. 'How can you help us?'

'Edda, come on,' says the baker. 'He's just a meddler.'

'I have seen your son.'

'What? Is he OK?' says Edda, grasping her husband's arm.

The baker begins to untie his apron, but the knot is too tight. 'Where did you see him? Why hasn't he come home?'

'He is in a house in Via dei Lussi,' says the detective. Then, looking in the corner at the empty stool, he adds, 'He's safe.'

The baker stops fidgeting with his apron. 'Via dei Lussi?' he says quietly.

Edda shakes her head. 'What's he doing there?'

'He's not a prisoner. He appears unharmed. Is there any reason why Davide would have gone there on his own?'

The baker slams his hand down on the counter. '*Fatti gli affari tuoi.*' *Mind your own business.*

'Jacopo, *basta*,' says Edda. 'Let me think.'

'What's there to think about? Via dei Lussi. *Hai capito?*'

She pushes her back against her husband and looks the detective square in the eyes. 'I don't know who you are, but now is not the time to talk. Come back tonight.'

'Edda?' The baker grabs his wife by the shoulders, but she brushes him off and steps towards the detective.

'After dark, ten o'clock,' she says. 'We live in the apartment above.'

Her husband touches a hand to his wound. 'Edda, what are you doing?'

'Wait across the street. I'll give you a sign from the window. Come around the back and wait.'

Then she strides past him and opens the door. 'Now, please go.'

The baker's hands drop to his sides, and he walks slowly back to the kitchen.

The detective doffs his cap and leaves.

On returning to Via Paolo Lomazzo, he retires from his sweep's job, much to the disappointment of the old man who was enjoying the easy life, and easy money.

Eleven

D ressed in overcoat, derby, and double soled shoes, the detective returns that evening at the decided hour and waits across the street from the bakery. Edda stands at the window of their apartment above. She doesn't seem to recognise him. He waves casually and touches the brim of his hat. She disappears.

The window opens, and she appears again, shaking out a tablecloth. She nods in his direction. Then, with the shutters drawn, she is gone.

He goes down the alley beside the block. A black cat darts from his path and hides amongst a pile of wooden crates. A side door opens into a dark passage and Edda, holding a candle, ushers him inside. She lights their way up the staircase.

'Did you see anyone on the street?'

'You mean Rizzo?'

'He's dangerous. He watches us even when we think he is gone. And he is not the only one.'

'The Mafia have a talent for being everywhere and nowhere at the same time.'

She looks back, her grave expression lit by the candlelight. People in the southern parts of Italy do not use the words

Mafia or Camorra so freely. Doing so has consequences. Instead, they call their oppressors Friends. Or, better yet, they say nothing.

On entering the apartment, Edda touches the mezuzah fixed at an angle on the doorpost, then kisses her fingers. It occurs to him that Levita is a Jewish name. Having seen the picture of the saint hanging in their bakery, he'd assumed they were Catholics.

Jacopo sits at a small, round dining table. He too does not seem to recognise their guest, and he stands as if Don Vito himself were entering his home. The detective removes his derby, and his host realises his mistake and sits down again.

'It's you,' he says.

'Jacopo, *per favore*,' says Edda. She takes the detective's hat and coat. 'Have a seat, Signor Saulino.'

Nursing his brow, the baker watches him closely as he sits at the table.

Edda goes to the cabinet and takes out a bottle.

'Will you have some wine?'

'If you'll both join me.'

'Edda, *che fai*?' says the baker. 'What are we drinking to?'

'Jacopo, *per favore*, fetch the glasses.'

He stands reluctantly and goes into the kitchen. Doors open and shut with a clamour. It seems the baker's profession comes with heavy hands.

'He means well,' says Edda, looking at her guest as if she could read minds.

The baker returns with three small glasses, like those used for serving sherry, and sets one down before each of them. 'So, out with it?' he says.

'I'm here to stop these people.'

'Stop them?' says the baker, slamming his hands on the table. 'They can't be stopped. They're like the plague.'

Edda puts a reassuring hand on her husband's shoulder, and he sits down heavily.

'Our family left Naples to get away from them,' she says, pouring the wine. 'Our business was simpler then. Jacopo baked at home, and we sold everything from a cart.'

'We barely got by,' says Jacopo.

'But we still saved,' says Edda, 'a little each week, and when we had enough, we came north.'

'Only we didn't get away,' Jacopo says, reaching for his glass. 'We thought our prospects would be better in Milan. But with business, come friends.' He raises his glass. '*Salute, ai nostri amici.*' He drinks, but without enjoyment.

'How can you help us?' says Edda.

'Tell me about the delivery service.'

Jacopo looks at his wife, and she reaches for his hand.

'The shop started well,' the baker says. 'We knew what we were doing.'

'Jacopo's traditional bakes brought a lot of customers. Immigrants like us. But then, well, as Jacopo said before, the Friends weren't far behind. They said they could protect us.'

'Who?'

The baker and his wife exchange glances and nod in agreement.

'His name is Giovanni Pappalardo,' says Edda.

The detective takes the cufflink from his pocket.

'Where did you get that?' says Jacopo.

'It was at the crime scene.'

'The one in the paper the other day?' asks Edda.

'And why were you there?' says Jacopo. '*Ascolta*, you haven't told us who you are?'

'I'm someone you can trust.'

The baker raises his eyes to the ceiling. '*Non mi fido di nessuno.*'

Edda picks up the cufflink and examines it closely. 'You think Pappalardo killed that man?' she says.

'If I can prove it, then he will go to jail. Tell me more.'

'Pappalardo presented himself as a businessman,' says Edda. 'A unionist interested in protecting local shop owners.'

'But we knew what he was,' says Jacopo. 'It was obvious even before that Sicilian *bastardo* showed up.'

Edda caresses her husband's cheek with the back of her hand. He looks away.

'We pay,' she says. 'We don't have a choice. But we're struggling, we barely cover our rent.'

'The delivery service,' says the detective, 'was that Davide's idea?'

'You saw yourself how much that bicycle means to him,' says Edda.

'It's all he thinks about,' says Jacopo. 'He said the delivery service was a way to make extra money. And he could get away from the bakery.'

'That too, perhaps,' says Edda. 'But it was a great success. Only Pappalardo heard about it, and, well, he had his own ideas.'

'Davide wouldn't do it. But they threatened us.'

'How does it work?' says the detective.

'Davide is given a list by Rizzo,' says Edda. 'He visits these men as he does other customers. They pay him what they owe Pappalardo.'

'Owe him for what?'

'We don't know,' says Edda. 'Davide says these men are involved in drugs.'

'They're addicts,' says Jacopo. 'He says they live like wild animals.'

'What happens if they don't pay?'

'Davide makes a mark next to their names on the list. In the evening Rizzo arrives and takes the old list and gives Davide a new one. That's all we know.'

'And the money?'

Edda shakes her head.

'I take the money to Pappalardo every Friday evening,' says Jacopo.

'Why doesn't Rizzo collect it?'

'He's too well known by the police,' says Edda.

'Not all of the *sbirri* are in the pocket of the Friends,' adds her husband. 'I take the money we owe for their so-called protection and the money Davide is paid during his visits.'

'How much?'

'A lot,' says Jacopo.

'Aren't you afraid of being robbed?'

'Nobody steals from the Friends,' says the baker. 'You'd be crazy to try. Besides, we're watched. The petty thieves fear Rizzo, more than they fear the police.'

'What's the set up inside the house?'

'It belongs to Pappalardo's mother. At least, I think so. She lives there, and it looks like the family home. She is harmless, doesn't seem to have her wits about her.'

'Who else is there when you drop off the money?'

'Pappalardo and Rizzo, then there's the guard at the door.'

The detective recalls the strongman and his roses. 'And that's it? Nobody else? What about the kid, Bonifacio?'

'He's new. Never saw him before this morning.'

'And that's it?'

'There was another man there once. I had the impression he was the boss. He didn't say anything. He just sat there. But seemed to run things. You know? A man of respect.'

The detective leans forward. 'Is there anything else you can tell me about this man?'

'For one thing, Pappalardo acted differently. He wasn't his usual arrogant self. And he seemed almost grateful for once that I had the money, that all his *spacciatori* paid that week without any trouble. The man could easily have passed for nobility, he dressed well, with his cashmere suit and fancy black Borsalino fedora. As I said, a man of respect. And he clearly felt disgusted by Pappalardo, like he would cut him like a pig if he was given reason to.'

'Jacopo, *per favore*,' says Edda.

'*È la verità.*'

The detective grips the stem of the glass between his fingertips, turning it slowly on the polished wood, then he downs the wine. 'I need to get inside,' he says.

The baker shakes his head. 'That's not going to happen.'

'I'm going to come with you.'

'*Ma sei matto?* No. They'll kill us all.'

'I have a plan. Tomorrow I'll start working for you.'

'No. No. No,' says the baker, bringing his fist down on the table, upsetting the glasses. 'The wine's gone to your head.'

'*Ascolta un attimo,*' says Edda, resting her hand on her husband's chest. 'Go on.'

'When Rizzo comes by tomorrow you introduce me as your cousin from Naples. I speak your dialect. It's believable.'

'*Oh Dio,*' says Jacopo, running his hands through his hair.

'You tell him I'm here to help out, because, well, with Davide not being there, and also your eye. *Una mano in più.*'

'Rizzo isn't a fool.'

'You're right. But it's good for business. The Sicilian will understand that. Bad business is bad news for the bosses, his bosses.'

'I don't know.'

'Rizzo and the kid will get used to me being around, I'll gain their trust, then when the next drop off comes, I can accompany you. And you'll introduce me to this Pappalardo.'

'That's tomorrow. It's too risky,' says Jacopo. 'He won't like it.'

'We could try,' says Edda, taking her husband's hand, but he snatches it away.

'We want our son,' he says. He drinks, but his hand begins to shake and wine spills from the glass. He sets it down and covers his eyes.

The detective glances around. Their home, furnished with only what is necessary, is kept neat and made warm with framed photographs, the family in happier times. He straightens his back against the chair and sighs. 'This might not be easy for you, but I need to ask. Rizzo mentioned earlier that your son is working for them, what do you think he meant?'

The baker shakes his head, staring across the room as if his mind were far away and he had not heard the detective speak. His wife lowers her hands in her lap, her expression strained. Then, gripping the sides of her chair, she says, 'Signor Saulino, there's something you should see.'

The baker scrapes his chair back. 'Edda?'

'We must trust him. Come with me,' she says.

She gets up and he follows her into the next room, while her husband remains at the table, staring at his glass.

The room is small, no more than a storage space. There is a bed and side table. On the wall, tacked up around a map of the Giro d'Italia race route, are pictures and newspaper clippings of Luigi Ganna and other professional bicyclists. Edda wraps her arms around herself and takes in the room, as if she, too, were seeing it for the first time.

'After Davide proved himself reliable,' she says, 'I mean, it was all his initiative, then Rizzo began offering him extra money. I caught him a few times.'

'To do what?'

She bites her lip, holding back tears. Then she kneels beside the bed. From under it, she takes out an elongated wooden box.

'What's this?'

'It belonged to my husband's father. He fought in Africa.' She runs her hand across the surface of the box. 'He referred to it affectionately as his *coscia d'agnello*. My husband never liked guns, so it was Davide's inheritance.'

She opens it.

'It's empty,' he says.

Placing her left hand inside the box, she lowers the lid.

'Davide was gone when we woke up this morning. I found the box under his pillow. He hadn't slept in his bed.'

Twelve

The detective arrives at the bakery before dawn. In his role as the baker's cousin, he'll use the name Simone Levita. He's done his best to, once again, reinvent himself. For the first time in years, he's left off shaving. And with no hat covering his short, unruly tufts of hair, and with his feet squeezed into a pair of cheap moccasins, he feels closer to the ground than usual.

For once the baker greets him warmly and provides him with the necessary garb, including a white apron and a pair of cotton trousers, which fit around the waist but are too long in the leg. Jacopo explains his morning routine, giving the newcomer a brief lesson in the fundamentals of baking bread. As the loaves come out of the wood oven, Edda brings the trays to the front of the shop. As the smell of warm bread fills the bakery, memories of his childhood in Padula waft through his mind.

Then, assisting Edda, he carries a pail outside and, using a rag and old newspapers, sets about cleaning the front windows. Bonifacio doesn't arrive until after seven. Edda glares at him as she comes out with the first bundle. The kid leans on the handlebars of the bicycle, smoking a cigarette. She waits for him to move away from the basket.

'You're too young to smoke,' she says.

'*Ma sta' zitta*,' he says, snatching a loaf from the bundle and biting off a chunk.

'Those are for the customers.'

'*Certo*,' he says. 'Give 'em here. You're making me late.'

The detective drops the rag into the pail and stands beside Edda.

'And who's this?' says the kid, sizing him up.

'This is my husband's cousin,' she says.

'*Piacere*,' says the detective, doing his best to smile and put the kid at ease.

The kid seems non-fussed. '*Ho capito*,' he says and pushes the bicycle into the street. 'Be ready later. I've better things to do with my day.' He walks slowly up the hill, eating the stolen loaf, until he reaches level ground, and only then does he get up onto the saddle and ride away.

Work is steady all through the morning, and although the newcomer is only responsible for the menial chores of kneading dough, greasing tins, and carrying trays back and forth, he is enjoying the work, and for a brief moment he loses himself in the joys of completing tasks without having to think too much.

The spell is broken in the late afternoon when Rizzo arrives. Not raising the suspicion of the Sicilian will be more difficult than fooling the kid. As usual, the wiry man takes his seat at the single table outside Tullio's bar. The waiter brings him his espresso and white wine.

When Bonifacio returns from another delivery, he wastes no time in telling Rizzo about the newcomer. The Sicilian calmly drinks his espresso before entering the bakery. He taps a cigarillo on his silver case.

'What's going on?' he says.

'Rizzo,' says Edda, biting the end of her pencil. The newcomer empties a fresh batch of bread into the baskets behind the counter and then turns towards the Sicilian.

'I'm Simone,' he says, lowering the empty tray. '*Piacere.*'

Jacopo joins them. He is holding a rolling pin at his side. He hopes that the baker isn't going to lose his temper.

'Simone is family,' Jacopo says.

'We needed help,' says Edda.

'*Sì*, after yesterday,' says her husband, raising a hand to his eye, 'it's not easy.'

'He gets headaches,' says Edda. 'Also, David isn't – '

'Davide?' says the Sicilian, putting the cigarillo back into the case. 'But you have Bonifacio.'

At the window, the kid perches on the bicycle, cleaning his fingernails with his knife.

'*Una mano in più,*' says the newcomer. 'It's good for business, no?'

The Sicilian regards him carefully, and then, brushing his moustache, he smiles slyly. 'Good for business, *dici?*' he says. 'I'll speak to the boss.'

'And Davide?' says Edda.

'What do you want me to tell you?'

Suddenly the kid whistles loudly, then pedals away. From across the street two policemen approach the shop. The Sicilian acts fast.

'Bread, *subito*,' he says.

'*Che cosa?*' says Edda.

'Bread,' he says calmly, 'give me some bread.'

She slips a loaf into a bag and hands it across the counter. As the police officers enter the shop, Rizzo turns casually and leaves. The men take no notice of the Sicilian. Instead, ensuring that there are no other customers, they stand guard at the door, speaking to each other in low voices.

'How can we help?' asks Edda.

But she is ignored. Soon enough, Chief Inspector Cattaneo strides in attended by the officer with the stiff lampshade moustache. On recognising the detective, Cattaneo moves to confront him, but suddenly stops in his steps. Instead, he turns towards Edda.

'We're looking for Davide Levita, he is your son, no?'

Edda steadies herself on the counter. 'My son?' she says, her voice faint.

'Our son is not here,' says Jacopo.

The inspector scrutinises the baker's bruises. 'What happened there?' he says.

The baker covers his eye with his hand. '*Niente.*'

'He fell in the kitchen,' says the detective.

Cattaneo shoots him a hard look. 'That right? And who are you supposed to be?'

'I'm a relative.'

'Relative, eh?'

'What do you want with our son?' says Edda.

'We need to speak with him.'

'We've not seen him,' she says, glancing at the detective and her husband.

'You don't know where he is?'

Edda, with her eyes towards the window, shakes her head.

'What's this about?' says Jacopo, tightening his grip on the rolling pin.

Cattaneo looks at the officer beside him who observes the scene with hawk eyes.

'Sergeant Bruno, *prego*,' says the inspector.

'There was a serious crime committed,' says the sergeant, taking a small notebook from his pocket. 'Your son Davide was reported seen leaving the address in question.'

The baker looks at his wife.

'Our son,' says Edda, 'he does deliveries all over the city.'

'I see,' says the sergeant, referring to his notebook. 'After midnight, Signora?'

'*Non è possibile*,' says Jacopo, moving towards the sergeant. The detective puts a hand on the baker's shoulder.

'Can you account for your son's whereabouts?' Cattaneo asks.

'Of course,' says Jacopo.

'Given that you don't know where he is now,' says the sergeant, tapping his notebook.

The baker brushes the detective aside and squares up to the policeman.

'My son is not a criminal.'

The sergeant places his hand firmly on the baker's chest. 'We didn't say he was.'

'Signor Levita, I suggest you calm down,' says Cattaneo.

The detective stands behind the baker, getting a good hold on the rolling pin.

'Jacopo, *per favore*,' says Edda.

'Do you possess a gun of any kind?' The inspector addresses this question to Edda, who is clearly in more control of her feelings.

'No, no gun,' she says. She places her hands over the ledger.

'And might Davide be in possession of one?' says the sergeant, looking the baker square in the eyes.

'*Basta*,' says Jacopo, lashing out with his hand, knocking the man's notebook to the floor.

The detective is quick to snatch the rolling pin away, but he cannot stop the sergeant from grabbing the baker by the elbow and pushing him against the wall, twisting his arm up behind his back.

'We warned you,' says the sergeant, spitting his words.

'Not my son, *è mio figlio*,' says the baker, struggling to free himself from the sergeant's hold.

The inspector gives the detective an exhausted look. 'Right, take him away,' he says to the men at the door.

Edda edges forward along the counter to the front of the shop. '*Dio mio*, Jacopo.'

The two officers surround the frantic baker, restraining him while the sergeant cuffs him.

'Wait,' says the detective.

'No,' says Cattaneo, raising his voice. 'Unless you want to answer a few questions yourself, I suggest you leave things alone.'

The sergeant retrieves his notebook from the floor and adjusts his uniform. The police officers march the subdued baker out the shop. He does not look at his wife, but glances back at the detective.

'Signora, my apologies,' says the inspector to Edda. 'If you should hear from your son, please tell him it'd be better if he presents himself to us.'

He goes to the door and then turns and points at the detective. 'I hope you know what you're doing.'

Thirteen

Armed with the rolling pin, the detective strides towards the door. In the mood for breaking heads.

'Wait,' says Edda, stepping in his path, pressing her back to the door. 'What is it with you men?' She takes the rolling pin from him and then locks the door.

'I'm sorry,' he says, loosening his apron string.

'There's no time for sorry, Signor Saulino,' she says. 'They have taken my husband. And my son. What am I going to do?'

He lowers his eyes and turns away. A path of flour covers the floor all the way to the kitchen. His footprints mixed up with those of the baker.

'The drop off is this evening,' she says.

'I'll go.'

'It'll be dangerous.'

'We'll close up, then go home. Expect me at nine. Have the money ready.'

She nods, tapping the rolling pin in her hand like a nightstick. He reties the apron and walks to the kitchen.

'Where are you going?' she says.

'To clean up.'

Back in his room, he reads an article in the *Milan Gazette* about the benevolence of Giovanni Pappalardo, the self-made businessman, who is quoted to have said that the rise of privately owned Chinese businesses in Milan is forcing Italians to leave their own city. To aid Italian shop owners, Pappalardo presents himself as a benefactor willing to fund small businesses by providing loans. But, as in the case of the Levita family, with Pappalardo's vested interest in the business, comes his protection. And a taking of the profits, whether there happen to be any or not.

He cuts the picture of the smug-faced Pappalardo from the paper and tacks it behind his door, adding to the pyramid of photographs, mugshots, and cuttings from newspapers: previous arrests, trials, deportations. From New York to Palermo. Giuseppe Morello, Ignazio Lupo, Giuseppe Fontana, Tommaso Petto. At the top of the pyramid sits Don Vito Cascio Ferro. On his right and left, Carlo Costantino and Antonino Passananti.

Compared to Don Vito, this Giovanni Pappalardo is a small fish. He plans to fry him all the same. But not before he extracts the information he needs. And if that requires a little bit of gutting, then he's no stranger to blood and entrails.

He considers changing his clothes, but he needs the Sicilian and the kid to recognise him. So much depends on secrecy. If only he'd understood that from the beginning.

When he set out from New York on February 9th, his mission had been clear, but not for that reason any less complicated, or dangerous. Initiating a secret information network on the activities of the Sicilian Mafia, a network that would be in direct contact with the NYPD, but without the knowledge of Italian law-enforcement agents, was an operation bordering on espionage. But it's success would see the end of the surge of criminal elements immigrating to the US. In other words, he'd come to cut the Black Hand off at the wrist.

The operation was to be conducted in utmost secrecy, even within the NYPD. Days before his departure, word spread amongst the force, and, no doubt, the criminal underground, that Lieutenant Petrosino had fallen ill and was under doctor's orders to take a lengthy leave of absence. He'd also been issued with a new passport under the assumed identity of a Jewish businessman. His name, Simone Velletri.

He opens his drawer, takes out his watch, and slips it into his breast pocket. It saved him once before, who's to say luck won't hit the same spot twice. Against better judgement, he picks up the picture postcard. Addressed to Mrs. Adelina Saulino Petrosino.

A kiss for you and my little girl, who has spent three months far from her daddy.

He never had a chance to send it. And now it's too late. Ghosts rattle chains, they don't send postcards. He slips it under his badge and slides them as far back into the drawer as they'll go. If he were given to listening to the voice inside his head, he would believe his old self to be lost. Officially dead to almost everyone who knew him. Dead to the very people he loves most.

He cleans his gun and loads it. He would prefer not to have to use it. Gunfire and dead bodies draw attention. He needs backup and someone to take away the trash once he's put it out for collection. If he calls Cattaneo, no doubt the stubborn chief inspector will want to do things by the book. He himself knows the book inside out but got rid of it long ago, because cunning criminals have read it, too, studying all the plot holes for them and their lawyers to escape through.

He searches his overcoat pocket for the calling card of the journalist. He still remembers the words of Sergeant Vachris the day he boarded the *Duca di Genova*. As they shook hands and embraced at the foot of the gangway, his friend had said, 'Watch out, boss. Down there everything's Mafia.' There and then, he'd made a promise to himself. *Trust no one*. But it's a promise he finds difficult to keep.

Inchiostro will be grateful for the headline. Together with the man's number, he finds the gold cufflink and pockets it.

He makes the call from the phone in the lobby.

'Signor Velletri?' says Inchiostro. 'I didn't expect to hear from you.'

'I need a favour.'

'Let me hear it.'

Hanging up, he senses he's being watched. The rich scent of cigarette. The swish of her long gown.

'Madam Xuan,' he says, brushing down a tuft of hair at the back of his head.

'Please,' she says, 'call me Xuan.'

'Alright,' he says, 'Xuan….'

'That's it, Joe,' she says. 'Be careful.' A plume of white smoke rises from her lips, and she is gone.

He waits for Edda's signal outside the barbershop. On the window, the word *Barbiere* followed by a straight razor blade is done in gold-leaf lettering. He presses his face against the glass. Light coming from somewhere in the back fills the shop with a soft glow. There are two salon chairs, cushioned with oxblood red leather. On the dark wood countertop pairs of trimming scissors, combs and brushes, jars of oil, all lie neatly against the high mirror. There is light but no sign of the living.

Soon enough, Edda opens the curtains and then quickly draws them. When she greets him at the door with a gas lamp, her downcast eyes tell him something is wrong. As on the night before, she lights their way up the stairs. At the door, she touches the mezuzah and kisses her fingers. This same ritual the previous night had seemed as habitual and necessary as lighting a lamp before entering a dark room, but this evening the gesture appears to carry the intent of a prayer.

Once they are safely inside, she places the lamp on the table and faces him. 'I've changed my mind.'

'Edda,' he says, 'there is no other way.'

She turns and walks into Davide's bedroom, and he follows her. She sits on the bed, her shoulders hunched.

'We could call the police,' she says, searching the palms of her hands held in her lap.

'No,' he says. 'We can't do that.'

'That inspector,' she says, looking into his eyes, 'I saw how he spoke to you. He knows you.'

He pulls up a chair and sits down.

'Edda, what do you think the police will do?'

She shakes her head. 'I want Davide to be safe.'

'That's why we don't want to get these people excited.'

'That's exactly it. Rizzo can be reasonable,' she says, 'but you don't know Pappalardo.'

'I'll be careful.'

'No, that man,' she says, 'he's unpredictable.'

'I'm going to pay them their money and have a little chat and bring your boy home.'

She rests her hand on her son's pillow. 'You'll protect him, won't you?'

'As long as they get their money,' he says, 'Davide will be safe.'

'You'll bring my son home, promise me.'

He rises from the chair. She reaches beneath the pillow and pulls out a flour sack.

He looks at the wall beside the boy's bed, at the map, the tacked-up picture of Luigi Ganna.

'You will bring him home?' says Edda again, her voice no more than a whisper.

He nods, slipping his own pistol into the sack, beneath the money.

'I'll make my own way out,' he says.

Before leaving the apartment, certain that Edda cannot see him, he touches the mezuzah at the door and kisses his fingers. For luck.

Fourteen

I t is dark when he approaches the house on Via dei Lussi, but the heat of the day still clings to the evening air. The gardener, attending the roses in the dim light from the porch, gives him a warning look as he reaches the steps.

'I'm here to see Signor Pappalardo.'

'I don't know you. What's your business?'

'I'm from the bakery,' he says, holding up the flour sack.

There is no change in the man's expression. Clearly, he is just a guard dog. He whistles and the kid appears at the doorway.

'It's you,' says Bonifacio, smirking. 'I heard your cousin got taken in by the *sbirri*.'

He nods. 'Yes,' he says, 'unfortunately.'

'He should watch his temper.'

He nods again, then raises his eyes to the night sky.

'*Bravo*,' says the kid, '*Hai capito tu*.'

'*Allora*,' says the gardener, 'you know him?'

'It's OK, Luigi,' says the kid, opening the door.

'Wait,' says the gardener. 'What's in the sack?'

'It's the same as always,' he says, shrugging and looking at the kid.

'*Ma cazzo,* Luigi, what do you think it is?'

The gardener, squeezing his pruning scissors, waves the detective past. The kid must be related to someone with a lot more clout than Pappalardo.

He follows Bonifacio into the house. At a glance, it is much the same as any Italian middle-class home. In the lounge, a picture of the Madonna and family portraits hang on the walls. Just as the baker said, an old woman sits in an armchair. Despite the heat, she wears a shawl over her shoulders and a quilt covers her legs.

While the kid ignores the woman, he greets her.

'*Niente da vedere, niente da dire,*' she says in a strong Milanese accent. *Nothing to see, nothing to say.*

'Don't worry yourself,' says Bonifacio.

'*Niente da vedere,*' she says louder.

He taps his forehead. 'She's not all there,' he says. 'In the head, *hai capito?*'

He leads the way to the back of the house and then upstairs. A voice comes from behind a closed door at the end of the hall. The kid knocks.

'Wait here,' he says and goes into the room.

Alone, he quickly reaches into the bag, removes his .38 from beneath the money, and slips it under his shirt into the seat of his trousers. He couldn't have hoped for a better chance.

The door opens and Bonifacio returns. 'He'll see you now,' he says, 'but he isn't in the best of moods.' Then, reaching to his back pocket for his pack of cigarettes, the kid returns downstairs. '*A dopo.*'

Inside the room, the Sicilian greets him with a nod, locks the door, and sits down at a card table covered with organised stacks of money. A cigarillo burns in a glass ashtray beside a stained, empty demitasse. He regards the detective with benign curiosity and resumes counting the money.

The room must have once been the master bedroom, but there is no bed. In the corner sits an open liquor cabinet lined with bottles, glasses, and an icebox. In the far end of the room, Pappalardo stands over a foldout table fixing a *panino*. He's stripped down to just sleeper shorts and a vest. Sweaty patches of white skin glisten through the hair on his wide back. He dabs his fleshy face with a hand towel, but it remains moist, like the skin of a bullfrog. His suit is hung up on a hook on the door to what appears to be an en-suite bathroom. French doors lead to the balcony.

The detective raises the sack. 'I have it,' he says, speaking in Neapolitan dialect.

Turning around, Pappalardo grins and then takes a bite of his *panino*. '*Bravo*,' he says with a mouth full of food. 'Nervousness must run in the family. Relax. Rizzo, count it.'

The Sicilian extends his hand, but the detective places the sack on the table. Rizzo has to reach forward. He notices the revolver in the holster beneath the Sicilian's jacket.

'I heard you're helping out,' says the fat man.

'*Eh sì*, my cousin was arrested this afternoon.'

'I was told.' He crams the last of the *panino* in his mouth. 'Davide.'

The boy comes in from the balcony.

'Look who's here,' says Pappalardo.

The boy, holding his elbow, recognises him but seems to sense something amiss.

'Davidino, so much like your mother,' says the detective, raising his arms. 'Lucky you got your looks from her side of the family, eh?'

'You look well, *Zio*,' says Davide, allowing himself to be embraced, a quick, awkward kiss on each cheek, before moving back. The boy appears to be playing along.

Pappalardo studies their act closely. 'So, where've you been?' he says.

'Well, like the boy may have told you, I had some opportunities in America.' He says this hoping to make an impression on this so-called man of business.

'America,' says the fat man, grinning. 'You hear that, Riz? *America.*'

Rizzo draws on his cigarillo and raises his eyebrows.

'Davide, be a good boy and fix Pappa a drink. The boy first looks at the detective and then does as he is told, going across the room to the liquor cabinet. 'And don't forget the ice. I'm dying here.'

Pappalardo brushes the crumbs from his vest and shorts and then, wrapping the towel around his thick neck, he sits in an armchair, putting his feet up on a cushioned stool.

'Tell me more.'

'What do you want to hear?'

Pappalardo laughs, again looking over to Rizzo from whom he seems to need constant encouragement.

'The particulars,' he says, dabbing his face.

Davide returns with a drink with lots of ice. The fat man holds the glass up.

'Did you put any vodka with this?

'You said not to forget – '

'I know what I said.' He waves the boy away. 'Let's hear it,' he says, looking at the detective. 'The particulars.'

'Well, Little Italy,' he says, 'you heard of it?'

'What do you take me for?' He sips his drink loudly, then sets the glass on the side table next to him. 'What did you do in this Little Italy?'

'Well, you know.'

'No, I don't.' The boy attempts a retreat to the balcony. 'Davide, don't go away.'

'We're good here,' says Rizzo, stacking the money beside the other piles.

The fat man nods, then groans, scratching himself. 'Davide, my feet hurt.'

The boy looks down at the man's grotesque legs but does not move.

'Davide, remember what we spoke about.'

The boy nods and, going down on his knees, takes one of the man's feet and begins to massage it. He averts his eyes, looking instead towards the French windows.

'*Vai avanti*, New York, Little Italy. What did you do there?'

'*Beh*, I had a little shoeshine business.'

'Shoeshine?'

'You know, spit and polish, on the street out in front of the train station.'

'Good business?' asks Pappalardo, raising the glass and holding it against his cheek.

'Good enough, lots of people coming out the station, men off to make up with their wives and sweethearts. Make a good impression with buffed shoes.'

'So why did you come back?'

'You know how it is.'

'No, I've never been. You been to America, Riz?'

The Sicilian shakes his head and picks up a pack of cards from the table and starts to lay them out in a game of solitaire.

'How about you, Davide?' He nudges the boy in the chest with his foot. 'Other one.'

Davide wipes his hands on his shirt and takes hold of the other foot. His mouth held in a tight grimace, like his stomach has just turned.

'My father, he went to America,' says Pappalardo. 'Only he didn't come back. Made a success of things.' He removes the towel from around his neck and folds it in his lap. 'No,' he says, 'there's only one reason why people come back, and you don't seem the type.'

'What type is that?' says the detective.

Pappalardo laughs. 'Davide, does he look the type to you?'

The boy doesn't answer. He lets go of the man's foot, then presses his palms to his trousers.

'Who said you could stop?' says the fat man, giving Davide a kick.

'I can't,' says the boy.

Pappalardo shoots a look across to the Sicilian. 'You hear that, Riz?'

The Sicilian ignores him, laying down another card. The jack of hearts.

'Maybe there's something else you'd like to do for me.'

The fat man leans across to the side table. He opens the drawer and takes out a revolver. The Bodeo 1889. The old man Levita's *leg of lamb*. Gripping the barrel, like a man who has never killed for himself, Pappalardo holds the weapon out towards Davide.

The Sicilian keeps a nervous eye on the fat man and re-shuffles the pack of cards.

'No, shoeshine man,' says Pappalardo, 'people who come back from America usually have something to hide.' He leans forward and kicks the stool away with his heel. Davide is quick to his feet. 'This gun belongs to the Levita family. You recognise it?'

'*Certo*,' says the detective, '*mio vecchio zio* used it for scaring the cats away from the chickens.'

'But not for killing, eh?' says the fat man. 'Davide, show us, *cosa sai fare*.'

The Sicilian sets down the cards. 'Gio,' he says, '*non qui, a casa tua, a casa di tua madre.'* Not here, at your house, your mother's house.

'*Sono cazzi miei*,' he shouts, his eyes on the boy. *It's my fucking business.*

Shaking his head, Rizzo stubs out his cigarillo and then slowly takes out his gun and checks the rounds.

The detective finds himself bringing a hand to his breast pocket where he feels the slight bulge of his watch. 'Davide,' he says, 'your parents want you to come home now.'

'I'm sure they do,' says Pappalardo. 'You're a good boy, ain't you? Talented. Let's see if you can shoot straight this time.'

'*Pensaci bene,* Gio,' says the Sicilian. *Think carefully.*

'*Basta pensare,*' says the fat man, shaking the weapon at the boy. 'Take it.'

Davide waves the gun away. 'I don't want to anymore.'

Pappalardo slams the glass down on the side table. 'Do it.'

'*Sta calmo,*' says the Sicilian, getting slowly to his feet.

Davide cocks his head as he looks at the detective.

'Would you like to go home?' he says, giving the boy a reassuring nod. 'Do what he says.'

'*Hai capito, ragazzino,*' says the fat man, '*ascolta tuo zio.*' *Listen to your uncle.*

Davide takes the gun and weighs it in his hand.

'*Bravo, ora pensa alla tua famiglia,*' says Pappalardo. *Now think about your family.*

'Leave them alone,' says the boy, pressing the gun against his stomach.

'That's up to you, *mio caro,*' says Pappalardo, gripping the ends of the towel, twisting it into a tight cord. 'Tell us again, shoeshine man, why are you here?'

'For Davide,' he says, smiling at the boy.

'*Che cosa?*' says Pappalardo.

'I came to see my nephew win the Giro d'Italia.'

Davide turns and, with his dark eyes wide, stares at this man, his proclaimed *zio.*

'*Basta,* kill this *pezzo di merda,*' says the fat man, whipping the towel out in front of him.

Davide shakes his head, shutting his eyes to hide his tears. The Sicilian raises his gun but doesn't seem to know at whom to aim.

'Listen to Pappa, and it will all be OK,' says the fat man. 'Your family will be safe.'

The boy's hand trembles as, opening his eyes, he lifts the gun, pointing it ahead of him.

'That's it,' says the detective, reaching slowly for his .38. 'You can do it.'

The Sicilian, increasingly uneasy, points his gun at the boy.

'*Sì*, you can do it,' repeats the detective. 'If Ganna can, who's to say you can't.'

The boy nods, cocking the Bodeo.

'What are you talking about?' says the fat man, trying to push himself up from the armchair.

But the boy is no longer listening. He whips 'round and fires a single shot.

As the fat man falls back clutching his belly, two more shots are fired. Davide and the Sicilian fall to the ground.

Rizzo's legs twitch beneath the table, the fallen stack of cards scattering about his body, and then he is still. The detective lowers his gun and rushes to Davide. Beneath his white shirt blood rises across his chest. Kneeling beside him, he places his hand to the boy's cheek. There is nothing he can do. He closes the boy's eyes.

Sunk in the armchair, the fat man groans, clutching his bleeding gut. The detective gets up and stands over him, pressing his boots down hard on the man's bare feet. He stabs the .38 into his mouth. The barrel scrapes against his teeth.

He wants to feed the rest of his bullets down the fat man's throat.

'Don Vito,' he says. 'Tell me where he is.'

The fat man stares wildly, whimpering, trying to speak. He takes his gun out the man's mouth.

'*Cazzo, aiutami*,' he says, gasping.

'Don Vito,' he repeats, cocking the gun.

Suddenly Bonifacio is at the door, knocking frantically. 'Rizzo?'

The fat man reaches out a bloodied hand. '*Aiutami*,' he says, but his voice is no more than a rasping whisper.

Bonifacio calls out once again and then can be heard re-treating down the stairs. The detective smacks the fat man across the side of the head with the back of his hand, then, moving across the room, he throws open the French windows. The gardener and the kid make their getaway down the street, each of them running in different directions. With the Sicilian dead, they clearly don't fancy their chances.

Again, he stands over the fat man. The sweat on his pale face looks cold. His expression is no longer only one of pain but of fear.

'Don Vito?' he asks again.

'*Vai al diavolo*,' says the fat man, trying his best to laugh, but blood trickles from the side of his mouth. '*Chiamami un'ambulanza, cazzo. Vuoi denaro?*' *Do you want money?*

The detective glances back at the boy, his strong limbs lifeless, all that spirit gone. He uncocks his gun and puts it away.

'*Lo sapevo*,' says the fat man, with a weak grin. *I knew it.* 'You all want money in the end. *Quanti?*'

The detective takes the cufflink from his trouser pocket. 'Recognise this?' he says, grabbing the fat man's cheeks, forcing him to open his mouth. More blood spills as he gasps for air. 'Don Vito?'

The man blinks helplessly and tries to shake his head, placing a bloodied hand on the detective's chest.

'*Va bene*,' he says, 'but you can keep your money.'

He shoves the cufflink down Pappalardo's throat, then covers his mouth and nose firmly. As the fat man chokes his eyes bulge. Clawing, then gripping the detective's shirt, his legs kick out feebly until, with a final desperate gasp, his beady eyes dilate into black globes.

The detective removes his hand, and the man's multiple chins slump to his chest, more blood spilling as his thick, white tongue lolls out his gaping mouth. He picks up the dirty towel, wipes the blood from his hands, and drops it over the dead man's head.

He kneels again besides Davide. He lifts the boy's hand and removes the Bodeo from his grip. He would like to take Davide home to his mother, but not like this. Inside his shirt pocket, he finds the signed picture of Luigi Ganna.

He puts the revolver in the sack with as much money as he can and goes downstairs.

The old woman has not moved from her chair. '*Niente da vedere*,' she says in a quiet voice. '*Niente da dire.*'

Outside he hears the approach of the distant police bell.

The journalist runs to him from across the street. 'I made the call as soon as I heard the shots,' he says, retreating from the detective's bloodied clothes. 'What the hell happened?'

'I wasn't here,' he says, going down the steps.

Against the fence, in the shadow of the rose bushes, he sees Davide's bicycle. He drops the sack in the basket, gets on the white saddle, and pedals away. Along with the clanging of the bell, footsteps come running up the sidewalk. But he is already far away. Safely hidden amongst the shadows of the cypress trees.

Fifteen

While light rain falls the next morning, the sticky heat is no less oppressive. He waits sheltered under the red canvas awning of the barbershop. The bamboo Venetian blinds drawn down. Across the street, the bakery is shut. Two police officers stand guard outside. Another at the corner of the alley, where Davide's bicycle rests, exactly where he'd left it the night before.

Edda looks down from the window. Her hair is loose and unkempt. She seems to look right through him, as if he didn't exist. He'd tried to tell her himself. But the police had got to her first. He takes a Toscano cigar from his pocket and chews on the end of it, until it's nothing but a brittle, mushy mess.

It is late evening before the police officers are relieved from their posts, and Chief Inspector Cattaneo and Sergeant Bruno appear, leaving the street entrance to the apartment. With a haggard scowl on his face, Cattaneo looks more troubled than usual. He spots the detective and his frown lines deepen.

He considers approaching the inspector. But, having gathered his men, Cattaneo gets into his automobile and leaves.

He continues to wait for a sign from Edda. None comes. Daylight fades, but no light shines in the apartment window. As he walks home, a thunderstorm breaks.

He is soaked to the bone by the time he reaches his room. His wounds ache when it rains, setting off memories. He does his best to ward them off, avoiding the faces of the men tacked on his door. But the harder the rain falls, the more vivid that night becomes, those three men dragging him back to the verge of death.

Back to that Friday evening....

When the heavy downpour finally let up over the streets of Palermo, he had decided to dine at the Cafè Oreto. He'd worn his dark suit, black shoes, and a dark grey overcoat. Around his neck, he wore his brown silk necktie, the one Adelina had given him as a parting gift. In the breast pocket of his waist-coat, he kept his gold watch on a chain. He picked up his .38-caliber Smith & Wesson from his yellow-leather suitcase, but then put it back beneath his vests. He never liked taking his gun to dinner. It weighed on his mind and gave him indigestion. Besides, there'd be no need. He put on his derby, grabbed his umbrella, and left the Hôtel de France.

The bar at Cafè Oreto was crowded with people drinking, but the restaurant was quiet. He was served by Geraci, his usual waiter. The lad was polite and friendly, and he didn't hover around the table making a fuss in hope of a big tip. He

dined well: pasta with *sugo di pomodoro*, *pesce spada*, fried pota-
toes, pecorino cheese, fruit, and a half-litre of the house white
wine. It was the last time he ate with a good appetite.

He was peeling an apple with a cheese knife when Carlo
Costantino and Antonino Passananti came up to his table.
They said that they had information about the Don. He re-
plied he was up to his ears in information, but none of it led
anywhere. So, could they please let him eat *in santa pace*.

Passananti leant forward and whispered in his ear. 'The
Don is here, and he's willing to meet you. We'll be at the garden gate in five minutes. But he will not be there for long.'

The detective nodded, putting down the knife. About to
leave, Costantino tried to filch a pear from the table, but Passananti grabbed him by the wrist, shaking his head.

He remembered thinking: there are two types of criminals:
those who commit crime when expedient, and those who
cannot help themselves.

He asked for the bill. It cost him a mere 2.70 lire. He paid
three lire and left the change on the plate for Geraci.

Piazza Marina was empty and dimly lit by gas lamps. At
the centre of the piazza the Garibaldi Garden cast ghostly
shadows on the church across the street. San Giuseppe dei
Miracoli. The name of the church had seemed auspicious.

The gate to the garden was locked. He peered through the
iron fence, but the exotic plants grew close and thick creating
an impenetrable jungle that made him uneasy. From the ter-
minus of the Shukert Company came the muted voices of the
passengers quickly boarding the streetcar to escape the cold
evening air. He took his watch from his inner pocket. 8:45.

Had they changed their minds? He lit a Toscano cigar and read the advertisement posters on a nearby column:

Questa sera, 12 Marzo 1909,
alle 8, al Teatro Biondo
primo spettacolo di
Paule Silver
La star francese

Cuscini di pura lana
Da 1.75 a 2 lire

The three men came from the shadows of the church. Passananti, Costantino, and a third man, his face hidden beneath an elegant, black fedora. They came fast, and as he crushed the Toscano under his shoe, he wished he'd brought his Smith and Wesson. As the three men opened their coats and drew their guns, all he could do was raise his umbrella. All three fired at close range, and he swung his umbrella, knocking the revolver from Costantino. He felt the chill of the iron fence against his back and then lunged towards his attackers only to fall heavily to his knees. Passananti booted him down on his back. Then the man in the fedora stood over him, aimed for the heart, and fired.

As suddenly as they'd appeared, the men ran, escaping into the shadows of the piazza in the direction of Palazzo Partanna, to be swallowed by the dark alleys.

As he lay on the street, his grip on his umbrella was fierce, but he could not lift his arm. All he could do was stare at the cold, wet cobbles, a large Belgian revolver, and his hat, lying up against the advertising column, before Piazza Marina rushed into darkness.

He returns to the bakery the following day. And the day after that. Although there are no police, there is no sign of Edda or Jacopo. The shop does not open. Customers do not come to queue. Bad news doesn't take long to get around. Only the dog returns. It sits at the door. Its fur is wet from the rain.

Early the next morning, he is up in his room when he hears the rustle of Xuan's gown outside his door. He opens before she can knock.

'Joe,' she says, 'the Levita family, they're leaving.'

He nods and her lips part slightly as if she were about to say more, but she simply draws breath and leaves.

He grabs his coat and hat and is about to dash out when he stops. He kneels beside his bed and shifts the mattress aside. From the flour sack, he removes the revolver and what money he needs and then pulls the mattress back in place. He slips the bundled sack into his large pocket.

The day is grey, and still the light rain falls. Outside the bakery, Edda and Jacopo pack the last of their belongings, held in boxes and bundles, onto a mule drawn cart. The dog lies at the entrance to the shop, its head up, attentive to the couple's movements.

At the detective's approach, Edda squeezes her husband's hand and then crosses the street. Jacopo turns towards the bakery and taps his leg. The dog raises itself, wagging its tail, and goes to him.

Edda and the detective stand sheltered beneath the awning of the barbershop in which there is still no sign of life.

He removes his hat. 'I'm sorry.'

'We don't blame you,' she says, taking his arm. 'Just.... Well, there's nothing to say.'

'Where will you go?'

'Where can we go?' she says. 'We've lost everything. And they will come for us eventually. For now, we'll head out of town, further north.'

'What about America?'

She smiles at him, humouring him as one does dreamers.

He reaches into the deep pocket of his overcoat and takes out the sack.

'What's this?' she says.

'Bread money.'

She stares hard at it, then is quick to hide it in her handbag.

'It's enough to get you to America. To get you started.'

'Edda,' says Jacopo, getting up onto the cart.

She looks back at her husband who places a *coppola* on his head and takes up the reins of the mule.

'Forgive him,' she says. 'He's hurting, and scared.'

'I understand,' he says. 'If anyone can convince him, it's you.' He takes the picture of the bicyclist from his inner pocket and puts it in her hands. 'Dreams aren't so bad if you have the opportunity.'

When she sees the picture, her face crumples, and she covers her eyes. Regaining herself, she puts the photograph safely beneath her blouse. Then she presses his arm tightly and returns to her husband.

He watches as the Levitas depart up the street. On the back of the cart, Davide's bicycle is tied securely with thin rope. Its white saddle gleaming in the grey, wet morning. The retriever follows, trotting alongside the mule. Jacopo holds the reins steady. And Edda, her hair now covered in a black headscarf, does not look back.

Acknowledgements

Joe Petrosino by Francis Russel is an authoritative account on the life and tragic death of Lieutenant Joseph Petrosino. It was an invaluable resource. Many thanks to my editorial team: Gwen Joy Uno, Fernando Dantas, Amy Suiter Clarke, Rachel McDonald. And special thanks to Hannes Pasqualini for the cover design on this series. Lastly, thank you to my family for their honest thoughts and encouragement along the way.

About the Author

Ryan Licata was born in Benoni, South Africa. He graduated from the University of Cape Town and later lived in the hills of Trentino, northern Italy. He earned an MFA at Kingston University, receiving the 2013 MFA Prize. He currently lives in Edinburgh, where he recently completed a Ph.D with a critical focus on the autobiographical fiction of J.M. Coetzee. Ryan's short stories feature in *The Ram Boutique Vol 1,* the Kingston University Press anthologies *Ripple* and *Writings,* and the literary magazine *Storgy.*

Printed in Great Britain
by Amazon

47235212R00061